FEUER AND MART

By Arrangement With Lester Linsk

present

NORMAN WISDOM

LOUISE TROY   GEORGE ROSE

in the New Musical

WALKING HAPPY

Book by
ROGER O. HIRSON & KETTI FRINGS

Lyrics by
SAMMY CAHN

Music by
JAMES VAN HEUSEN

with

ED BAKEY   GORDON DILWORTH   EMMA TREKMAN

GRETCHEN VAN AKEN   SHARON DIERKING

JAMES B. SPANN   MICHAEL BERKSON

Scenery and Lighting by
ROBERT RANDOLPH

Costumes by
ROBERT FLETCHER

Based on the play "HOBSON'S CHOICE" by Harold Brighouse

Musical Direction by
JULIAN STEIN

Orchestrations by
LARRY WILCOX

Dance Music Arranged by
ED SCOTT

Dances and Musical Numbers Staged by
DANNY DANIELS

Directed by
CY FEUER

Original Cast Album by Capitol Records

SAMUEL FRENCH, INC.

25 WEST 45TH STREET   NEW YORK 10036
7623 SUNSET BOULEVARD   HOLLYWOOD 90046
LONDON   *TORONTO*

WALKING HAPPY

Amateurs wishing to arrange for the production of *WALKING HAPPY* must make application to SAMUEL FRENCH, INC., at 25 West 45th Street, New York, N.Y. 10036, giving the following particulars:

(1) The name of the town and theatre or hall in which it is proposed to give the production.

(2) The maximum seating capacity of the theatre or hall.

(3) Scale of ticket prices.

(4) The number of performances it is intended to give, and the dates thereof.

(5) Indicate whether you will use an orchestration or simply a piano.

Upon receipt of these particulars SAMUEL FRENCH, INC., will quote the terms upon which permission for performances will be granted.

A set or orchestral parts with piano conductor score and principal chorus books will be loaned two months prior to the production ONLY on receipt of the royalty quoted for all performances, the rental fee and a refundable deposit. The deposit will be refunded on the safe return to SAMUEL FRENCH, INC. of all material loaned for the production.

CAST

(In order of appearance)

Henry Horatio Hobson	GEORGE ROSE
George Beenstock	ED BAKEY
Minns	THOMAS BOYD
Denton	CASPER ROOS
Tudsbury	CARL NICHOLAS
Heeler	MICHAEL QUINN
Maggie Hobson	LOUISE TROY
Alice Hobson	SHARON DIERKING
Vickie Hobson	GRETCHEN VAN AKEN
Albert Beenstock	JAMES B. SPANN
Freddie Beenstock	MICHAEL BERKSON
Mrs. Hepworth	EMMA TREKMAN
Footman	RICHARD KORTHAZE
Tubby Wadlow	GORDON DILWORTH
Will Mossop	NORMAN WISDOM
Ada Figgins	JANE LAUGHLIN
Mrs. Figgins	LUCILLE BENSON
The Figgins Brothers	IAN GARRY / AL LANTI
Customer	ELEANOR BERGQUIST
Handbill Boy	RICHARD SEDERHOLM

SYNOPSIS OF SCENE

The Scene is Salford, an industrial town in Lancashire, England.

The time is 1880.

WALKING HAPPY

ACT I

WALKING HAPPY

ACT II

The Moonrakers pub. Night. The pub
is filled with men, drinking and
noisy. At a downstage table are
HENRY HOBSON, TUDSBURY, DENTON, and
HEELER.

MINNS, the bartender's voice is
raised above the din.

                    MINNS
)rink up, gentlemen. Fifteen minutes to closing time.

                    HOBSON
⇒Minns, another round ...

                    MINNS
⊃oming right up, Henry ...

                    HEELER
Not for me, Hobson. I've got to be on my way.

                    HOBSON
⊃h, don't rush off yet, Heeler.

                    HEELER
You haven't got a wife waiting up for you ...

                    HOBSON
Nay, I'm bless that way. But even when my wife was alive,
there was only one master in my house.

                    DENTON
You do have the knack of dealing with females, Henry.

                    HOBSON
A tight rein, Denton. When my three daughters get frisky,
I pull back hard, and they settle down quick enough.

                    HEELER
You just wait till they get marriage on their minds, Henry,
then there's no controlling them.

                    HOBSON
Oh, that's begun already. But I'm not making my move until I
can find young men of real substance for them. I don't want
more porkers feeding out of my trough.

DENTON

With three girls to get rid of, you can't be too particula

HOBSON

Two ... Denton ... two.

DENTON

Two?

HOBSON

Aye ... the two youngest could go tomorrow. They're liabi
ties. But I'll hang on to my oldest girl, Maggie. She's
asset. She's my cook, housekeeper, stock clerk, bookkeepe
and my salesman. A valuable piece of property that one, a
I don't part easy with value.

(BEENSTOCK has entered. MINNS sees
him and rings the bell)

MINNS

Gentlemen ... gentlemen ... Mr. Beenstock is here. Mr.
Beenstock of the Blue Rosette Temperance Society. Direct
your attention please to his weekly message.

BEENSTOCK

Thank you, Minns ...

MINNS

Could you keep it short, Mr. Beenstock? There's gentlemen
here as much as a pint behind on their daily quota ...

BEENSTOCK

I'll do my best.
(Turns on the group)
You're all going to hell, you know that ... and only the bl
rosette can save you from eternal damnation.

HOBSON

Beenstock, I cannot understand why a thriving corn merchant
like you spends so much of his time spreading the devil's
gospel ...

BEENSTOCK

Temperance is not the devil's gospel, Hobson ...

HOBSON

It is to a man with a thirst ...

BEENSTOCK

Gentlemen, gentlemen, I know the devil lurks about whisperir
words of temptation in your ear. But I implore you to use
the will-power god gave you to sweep out the bad thoughts ar
sweep in the good. Remember, a clean mind is a pebble in
the devil's shoe. All right, gentlemen, ready to do battle.

Glasses down.

(THEY place glasses on board)

Eyes fixed.

(THEY stare ahead)

Contemplate the source of your debasement.

(SONG: "THINK OF SOMETHING ELSE"

ALCOHOL A LIQUID WHICH RESULTS FROM FERMENTATION
THE BOTTLING WHICH IS SATAN'S OCCUPATION
RESULTING IN THE USERS DEGRADATION
BEFORE YOU DRINK THAT DRINK
I BEG YOU STOP AND THINK
      (Speaks)
Think ...
      (Sings)
THINK OF SOMETHING ELSE
THINK OF SOMETHING ELSE
SKIP THAT DRINK AND
THINK OF SOMETHING ELSE.

MEN

THINK OF SOMETHING ELSE
THINK OF SOMETHING ELSE
JUST FORGET THAT DRINK

BEENSTOCK

AND THINK OF SOMETHING ELSE

MEN

AND THINK OF SOMETHING ELSE

BEENSTOCK
      (Speaks)
Think!

1ST MAN
      (Speaks)
Think of something else, like a --

BEENSTOCK

Well, like a ...

HOBSON
Let me help you, Mr. Beenstock.
      (Speaks in rhythm)
Peaceful dreams, cheerful waking
Waking without fingers shaking
Breaking fast on steady legs
Sausages and golden eggs
Home-made jams of which you boast
Marmalade to spread on toast!

                    MEN
Toast?

                    HOBSON
Aye, toast! Gentlemen, Her Majesty, Queen Victoria.

                    MEN
To the Queen!

                    BEENSTOCK
          (Sings)
ALCOHOL, A LIQUID WHICH RESULTS IN

                    HOBSON
          (Sings)
IN RELAZATION

                    BEENSTOCK
AND BRINGS ABOUT A MAN'S

                    HOBSON
EMANCIPATION
HE PLEADS US NOT TO DRINK
ALL RIGHT THEN LET US THINK

                    MEN
ALL RIGHT THEN LET US THINK

                    HOBSON
          (Speaks)
Really think!
          (Sings)
THINK OF SOMETHING ELSE
THINK OF SOMETHING ELSE
LET"S NOT DRINK AND THINK OF SOMETHING ELSE
THINK OF NAGGING WIVES, TONGUES LIKE BUTCHER'S KNIVES
SPONGING RELATIVES, WOES A DAUGHTER GIVES
DEBTS AND BILLS TO PAY, 'TIL YOU'RE LAID AWAY
WHEN YOU START TO THINK, THAT"S WHEN YOU NEED A DRINK

                    MEN
AND WHEN YOU HAVE THAT DRINK

                    HOBSON
YOUR TROUBLES START TO SHRINK

                    ALL
AND YOU BEGIN TO --
THINK OF SOMETHING ELSE
THINK OF SOMETHING ELSE
HAVE A DRINK AND THINK OF SOMETHING ELSE

                    -4-

FIRST GROUP	SECOND GROUP
THINK OF SOMETHING ELSE	THINK OF SOMETHING ELSE
THINK OF SOMETHING ELSE	AND HAVE YOURSELF A DRINK
HAVE A DRINK AND	THE BLOOMIN' TRUTH IS
THINK OF SOMETHING ELSE	THERE JUST AIN'T ANOTHER
	THOUGHT WE CAN THINK

                                    THINK OF SOMETHING ELSE
                                    AND HAVE YOURSELF A DRINK

THINK OF SOMETHING ELSE
THINK OF

                            ALL
IT'S VERY EASY
HAVE YOURSELF A, HAVE YOURSELF A,
HAVE YOURSELF A, HAVE YOURSELF A
DRINK
AND THINK OF SOMETHING ELSE.

                        MINNS
                (Ringing the bell)
Closing time, gentlemen ...

                        HOBSON
I'll have just one more, Minns.

                        MINNS
You wouldn't want me to break the law, would you, Henry?

                        HEELER
Come on, Henry ... Drink up.

                        HOBSON
Aye, and think of something else.

                HOBSON, DENTON, TUDSBURY, HEELER
        (Sing)
THINK OF SOMETHING ELSE   Piano Score No. 2A
THINK OF SOMETHING ELSE   Page 12
HAVE A DRINK AND
THINK OF SOMETHING ELSE

                (THEY continue singing as THEY leave
                the pub. The song carries them into
                the street in front of the Bootery)

                        HOBSON
Goodnight, lads. I'll see you in the morning.
                (HOBSON unlocks the door and
                goes into the bootery as the
                THREE MEN go upstage, singing,
                and off.
                        —5—

MUSIC and LIGHTS indicate a change
to morning as people begin to fill
the street going about their business
At this point, the Bootery opens)

Piano Score No.
Page 26

ACT I

Scene 2

> HOBSON's Bootery. MAGGIE enters,
> unlocks the door, pulls up the
> shade. ALICE and VICKIE enter.

VICKIE
Good morning, Maggie. Has father gone out?

MAGGIE
No, he hasn't.

ALICE
Oh, he is late this morning.

VICKIE
Has he had his breakfast yet?

MAGGIE
Nay, he hasn't. He was refreshing himself till very late
at the pub last night.

VICKIE
He'll probably need reviving.

ALICE
Well, I wish he'd go out and do it.

MAGGIE
Are you two expecting somebody?

VICKIE
Yes, we are, and we'll thank you to go when they come.

MAGGIE
And leave you two in charge of shop?

VICKIE
Maggie, it's bad enough father being so unreasonable about
Freddie and Albert. You'd think we'd have our own sister
on our side.

MAGGIE
Vickie, when it comes to choosing sides, I'll do what's right.
Meanwhile I'm responsible for what goes on in shop.

(ALBERT and FREDDIE enter)

ALBERT
Good morning, Miss Alice ... Miss Vickie ..

—7—

(MAGGIE nods cooly)

                    ALICE   VICKIE
Good morning, Albert.   Good morning, Freddie.

                              FREDDIE
Has your father gone out yet?

                              VICKIE
No, he hasn't come down ...

                              ALBERT
Well, in that case I think we'd better be on our way.

                              ALICE
Don't rush off.

                              FREDDIE
But your father may come down at any minute ...

                              VICKIE
I know, but we never have a moment together any more.

                              MAGGIE
And what can Hobson's do for the Beenstock brothers this
morning?

                              ALBERT
Oh, we just came in to look, Miss Maggie.

                              MAGGIE
This is a shop, not a museum.

                              FREDDIE
Oh ... well ... I'll have a pair of bootlaces, please ...

                              MAGGIE
What size do you take in boots?

                              FREDDIE
Eights. Does that matter to laces?

                              MAGGIE
It matters to boots. Number eights from the third rack,
Vickie. Sit down, Freddie.

                              VICKIE
Freddie didn't come in to buy boots, Maggie.

                              MAGGIE
Oh, I wonder why he does come in so often. Here, try these
on. Give me a hand.

                              FREDDIE
But, Miss Maggie, I don't want to buy them.

                              — 8 —

MAGGIE

Oh, these uppers are disgraceful for a tradesman to wear ...

FREDDIE

But, I really don't want to buy them.

MAGGIE

There, now, how does that feel?

FREDDIE

Very comfortable, thank you ... but I really don't want to buy them.

ALBERT

What's the price of those?

MAGGIE

A pound.

ALBERT

A pound!

MAGGIE

Aye ... I'll fit you with a pair next.

ALBERT

Nay, one pair in the family is quite enough.

FREDDIE
(Paying)

Well, if anyone had told me I was coming in here to spend a pound this morning, I'd have called him crazy ... a pound ...

MAGGIE

And one and six for the repair of your old shoes ... Vickie.

FREDDIE

Well, I didn't want these shoes. You saw what she made me do.

MAGGIE
(SHE has opened the door and
now turns to the BOYS)

Good morning, Freddie. Good morning, Albert ...

FREDDIE

Good morning, Miss Maggie ...

ALBERT

Good morning, Miss Maggie ...

(THEY look hopelessly at ALICE
and VICKIE and go)

VICKIE

Maggie, we know you're a pushing saleswoman, but ...

                    MAGGIE
That'll teach them to keep out of here. They have entirel
too much time on their hands.

                    ALICE
You know why they come.

                    MAGGIE
Aye, and it's about time they paid rent for it.

                    VICKIE
But if father won't let us go courting, where else can we
meet Freddie and Albert?

                    MAGGIE
If they want to wed you, why don't they declare themselves:

                    ALICE
Courting must come first.

                    MAGGIE
Not necessarily. You see the fancy buckle on this? Well,
courting before declaring is like this buckle. All glitter
and no use to anybody.

          (HOBSON enters)

Morning, father.

                    HOBSON
Good morning. Now don't stand about. There's plenty to do
I'm just going out for a quarter of an hour ...

                    MAGGIE
Isn't it a bit early for Moonrakers, Father ...

                    HOBSON
Moonrakers? Who said anything about going to the pub ...

                    ALICE
Oh, we know where you're going ...

                    VICKIE
And twice this week you stayed so long your dinner was ruine
...

                    HOBSON
It's two hours to dinner time ...

                    VICKIE
Time flies in Moonrakers, Father ...

                    HOBSON
Well, I'll be ...

                    — 10 —

ALICE

Don't swear, Father ...

HOBSON

No, I'll tell you some home truths instead. Now, listen to me ... Providence has decreed that you should lack a mother's hand at a time when single girls grow bumptious and must have somebody to rule. Well, I'll tell you this, you'll none rule me. You keep on this course of conduct, and I'll get rid of both of you.

### ALICE	### VICKIE
Get rid of us, father ...	Father ...

HOBSON

I'll choose a pair of husbands for you, my lasses ...

VICKIE

Why can't we choose husbands for ourselves ...

HOBSON

Thank God, we are not a heathen nation yet. Now, back into the house. There's my room to be made up.

> (ALICE and VICKIE go. HOBSON heads
> for the door)

MAGGIE

You're doing a lot of talking to Alice and Vickie, Father. Where do I come in?

HOBSON

You?

MAGGIE

Aye ... If you're dealing out husbands, don't I get one?

HOBSON

Well, that's a good one. You with a husband.

MAGGIE

Father, I'm serious.

HOBSON

Oh, you're serious, are you? Well, if you want the brutal truth, you are past the marrying age. You're a proper old maid if ever there was one.

MAGGIE

I'm only thirty.

HOBSON

Aye ... thirty ... and shelved for good.

— 11 —

                    MAGGIE
You say that as if it gave you satisfaction ...

                    HOBSON
Maggie, I'm just laying out the truth, and I know you can
face it ...

                    MAGGIE
Father, if we're dealing with truths, tell me something.
All those years I counted on you to find someone for me
... how hard did you look?

                    HOBSON
Now, Maggie ...

                    MAGGIE
The truth is ... you didn't look at all, isn't it? You
never wanted to find a husband for me.

                    HOBSON
Maggie ... that's nonsense. Haven't I always depended on yo
... given you my respect. I put you in charge of the house
... and the shop. I allowed you to raise Alice and Vickie.
That's quite a bit I've done for you. Now don't waste your
time dreaming about what you just can't have. And see that
the liver's not undercooked.
            (HE goes.

      MAGGIE SINGS: "WHERE WAS I?"   Piano Score No. 3
                                               Page 29
                    MAGGIE
VERSE:

THERE COMES A DAY, WHEN YOU HAVE TO FACE
THE TRUTH HOWEVER GRIM
AND ANGRY THO I AM IN THIS CASE
I'M AS ANGRY AT ME AS AT HIM

I SIMPLY KEEP WAITING AND GOING ALONG
INSTEAD OF DEBATING THE RIGHT OR THE WRONG
ATTENDING THE STORE AND KEEPING HIM FED
FOR WHICH MY REWARD IS A PAT ON THE HEAD

YOU'RE SHELVED HE SAID, AS HE TURNED TO GO
"THROUGH," HE SAID WANTING ME TO KNOW
"DONE" HE SAID, THAT'S THE WORD HE SPOKE
"MISSED YOUR CHANCE," SAID IT LIKE A JOKE

IT'S A SAD LITTLE JOKE WHICH I CAN'T DENY
BUT THE QUESTION IS, SHOULD I LAUGH OR CRY --

CHORUS:

WHEN ALL THE VERY YOUNG BOYS
THE VERY DASHING YOUNG BOYS

                    - 12 -

MAGGIE (Continued)

AME WISTFULLY WAND'RING BY
HERE WAS I? WHERE WAS I?

HEN ALL THE VERY YOUNG MEN
HE VERY HANDSOME YOUNG MEN
AME CALLING WITH HOPES HELD HIGH
HERE WAS I? WHERE WAS I?
OW GONE ARE ALL THE YOUNG BOYS
ND GONE ARE ALL THE YOUNG MEN
 DIDN'T DREAM, THEY'D EVER SEEM, SO SUBLIME

ND IF THEY'RE WOND'RING WHERE WAS I.
ELL THEM I WAS HERE -- ALL THE TIME!!!

          (After song, HOBSON enters)

                    HOBSON
laggie ... Maggie ... quickly ... Mrs. Hepworth's on her
vay in ...
          (HE crosses to door)
Alice ... Vickie ... shop ... shop ...
          (HE turns back to the shop door.
          MRS. HEPWORTH enters)
Oh, good morning, Mrs. Hepworth. What a lovely day ...

                    MRS. HEPWORTH
Good morning, Hobson. I've come about these boots you sent
me home!

                    HOBSON
They look very nice ...

                    MRS. HEPWORTH
Who made these boots?

                    HOBSON
We did, Madam. They're our own make.

                    MRS. HEPWORTH
But, who made them?

                    HOBSON
I'm responsible for all work on these premises ... Madam.

                    MRS. HEPWORTH
          (Turning to MAGGIE in irritation)
Young woman, you appear to have some sense. Can you help me?

                    MAGGIE
Oh, I think so.
          (MAGGIE steps forward and stamps
          twice on the floor)

                    — 13 —

                              HOBSON
You wish to see the identical workman, Madam?

                         MRS. HEPWORTH
Isn't that what I said?

                    (A trap opens and TUBBY WADLOW comes
                    up waist high. HE squints against the
                    glare of unaccustomed light)

Man, did you make these boots?

                    (TUBBY studies her shoes carefully
                    from his waist-high position)

                              TUBBY
They're Will's making, those.

                         MRS. HEPWORTH
Will?

                              TUBBY
Yes, mum.
                    (HE shuts the trap quickly and
                    is gone)

                         MRS. HEPWORTH
Who's Will?

                              HOBSON
Will Mossop, Madam.
                    (HOBSON stamps on the trap once and
                    angrily)
And, believe me, Madam, if there's anything wrong, I'll
make the man suffer for it ...

                    (The trap opens and a grimy boothand
                    emerges waist-high. HE is WILL MOSSOP,
                    in his early 30's)

                              WILL
Someone stomp for me?

                         MRS. HEPWORTH
My word, they're like rabbits.
                    (To WILL)
Did you make these boots?

                              WILL
                    (Peering at them carefully)
Yes, mum, I made them last week.

                              — 14 —

MRS. HEPWORTH

an, I want you to know that I'm very particular about
hat I put on my feet.

HOBSON

assure you, madam, it shall not happen again.

MRS. HEPWORTH

hat shan't?

HOBSON
(Crestfallen)
don't know.

MRS. HEPWORTH

Then hold your tongue.
(To WILL)
I have tried every shop from here to Manchester and these
are the best-made pair of boots I've ever had. Now, listen
carefully; in future, you'll make all my boots including
those for my family and for my entire staff.
(Turns to HOBSON)
You hear that, Hobson?

HOBSON

Yes, madam. Of course he shall.

MRS. HEPWORTH

The man's a treasure. Take that.

(WILL flinches, expecting a blow.
But SHE is holding out a visiting
card. SHE presses it on him)
Here, man, here.

(HE takes it and looks at it)

Can't you see what's on it?

WILL
(Puzzled)
Writing?

MRS. HEPWORTH

Well, read it.

WILL

I'm trying to, mum.

MRS. HEPWORTH

Bless the man. Can't you read?

WILL

I do a bit. Only it's such funny print.

(MAGGIE steps in and turns the
card right side up)

MAGGIE

It's the italics, Mrs. Hepworth, that gives him the proble
It's Mrs. Hepworth's card, Will.

WILL

Oh, I see ...
(HE starts to return her card)

MRS. HEPWORTH

You'll keep that card and if you leave here for another sh
you're to inform me immediately.

HOBSON

Oh, he won't make a change, Madam.

MRS. HEPWORTH

How do you know? I expect you underpay him.
(To WILL)
Does he?

WILL

I manage, mum.

MRS. HEPWORTH

In any case, you've got my card. Good morning, Hobson.

HOBSON

Good morning, Mrs. Hepworth. Very glad to have the honor
of serving you again.
(HE turns on WILL)
What you standing there for like half an idiot? Down ...
Mossop ... down ... down.

(WILL scurried down the steps)

I wish some people would mind their own business. Praising
a workman to his face. Undermining the whole social order.

MAGGIE

Oh, don't be silly, father. Mossop's a fine boothand.
He deserved it.

HOBSON

Maggie, there are people who wear clogs ... And there are
people who wear boots ... If the Lord meant them to mix
He wouldn't have given us two kinds of shoes. That's the
last time she sets foot in my shop, I give you my word.

VICKIE

Oh, father, you're just talking ...

VICKIE (Continued)
                    (To ALICE)
The day father turns away carriage trade, it'll be raining
guineas on the pavement ...

                         HOBSON
That's a bumptious remark, Vickie ... and I'll have no more
of it.

                         VICKIE
Yes, father ...

                         HOBSON
Now, back to work the pair of you.

                    (ALICE and VICKIE go. HOBSON
                    starts out)

                         MAGGIE   Piano Score No. 3A
Dinner's at one, father.   Page 35

                         HOBSON
Now, look here, Maggie, I set the hours in this house.
Dinner's at one o'clock becuase I say it's at one o'clock,
not because you say it's at one o'clock.

                         MAGGIE
Yes, father.

                         HOBSON
So long as that's understood, dinner's at one o'clock.
                    (HE goes. MAGGIE paces the floor a
                    moment, then stamps on the trap. WILL
                    MOSSOP comes up)

                         WILL
You stomped, Miss Maggie ... ?
                    (HE wipes his nose on his sleeve)

                         MAGGIE
                    (Startled)
Oh, no, Willie ... I didn't mean ...

                         WILL
Oh, but I thought you stomped ...

                         MAGGIE
Well, I did, but it wasn't for you. You can go, Will.

                    (WILL descends and closes the trap.
                    MAGGIE stands distracted for a moment,
                    then turns and looks at the trap. SHE
                    gets an idea, crosses to the trap and
                    stomps)
                         — 17 —

                        WILL
                (Appearing from the trap)
        Were that an official stomp, Miss Maggie?

                        MAGGIE
        Aye, Willie. Come on up here.

                        WILL
                (Looks at her questioningly)
        Into shop? Nay, I couldn't do that, Miss Maggie.

                        MAGGIE
        Why not?

                        WILL
        Well, I've never been all the way up before. It doesn't
        seem fitting somehow ...

                        MAGGIE
        All right. Stay where you are. But show me your hands.

                        WILL
                (Holds out his hands hesitantly)
        They're dirty.

                        MAGGIE
        Aye, they're dirty, but they're clever. They can shape
        leather like no other man's that ever came into this shop.
        Who taught you, Will?

                        WILL
        I learnt my trade where I were raised.

                        MAGGIE
        The workhouse ... ?

                        WILL
        Aye ... they wanted to give me a trade so that I'd not
        become a burthen to rate-payers ...

                        MAGGIE
        Well, you're a natural genius at making boots. It's a pity
        you're a natural fool at all else.

                        WILL
        Aye, I'm not much good at anything but leather. And that's
        a fact.

                        MAGGIE
        When are you going to leave Hobson's, Will?

                        WILL
                (Apprehensively)
        Leave Hobson's? But I thought I gave satisfaction ...

                    MAGGIE

You heard what Mrs. Hepworth said. The best boots from here
to Manchester. You know the wages a bootmaker like you
could get in Manchester ... in one of them big shops?

                    WILL

I'd be feared to go in them fine places. Anyway I'm used
to Hobson's.

                    MAGGIE

Do you know what keeps Hobson's on its legs, Will Mossop?

                    WILL

You do, Miss Maggie.

                    MAGGIE

The two of us. You're the best bootmaker in Salford and
I'm the best saleswoman ...

                    WILL

No question, you're a wonder in shop, Miss Maggie.

                    MAGGIE

And you're a marvel at bench. Well?

                    WILL

Well, what?

                    MAGGIE

Well, it seems to point one way to me.

                    WILL
          (Wary)
Which way is that?

                    MAGGIE

Oh, you're leaving me to do all the work, my lad.

                    WILL
          (Uncomfortable)
I'd best be getting back to my stool, Miss Maggie.
          (HE starts to lower the trap)

                    MAGGIE ,

You'll go when I'm done with you.

          (HE stops)

No come on up here ... no nonsense.

                    WILL

But I ...
          (HE comes up)

                              MAGGIE
All the way up.

                                        WILL
But I am all the way up.

                              MAGGIE
So you are.
                    (SHE looks him over carefully)

                                        WILL
What doest want me for?

                              MAGGIE
Turn around --

          (HE does. MUSIC starts)

Walk over there. Go on. Go on.

          (HE does. SHE beckons him back)

Yes. You'll do for me.

                                        WILL
                    (In a cold sweat)
I will ... ?

                              MAGGIE
Will Mossop, you're my man.

                                        WILL
                    (Panic)
I am ... ?

                              MAGGIE
You know what I see when I look at you?

                                        WILL
                    (Hysteria)
We're very busy in cellar ...

                              MAGGIE
A business. A rich, thriving business. My brains and
your hands 'ull make a working partnership.

                                        WILL
                    (Relief)
Oh, a partnership. Well, that's different. I'll have to
think that over, Miss Maggie.
                    (HE starts down the trap, then
                     comes back up again)
For a minute there I thought you were axing me to wed you.

                              -20-

MAGGIE

: am.

(WILL drops out of sight like
a stone, the trap door slamming
shut behind him. MAGGIE opens
it and calls down)

Will Mossop, you're calling on me Sunday.
(SHE listens, but there is no
answer. SHE calls loudly)
Will Mossop ... !

(WILL's head emerges cautiously
and HE holds the trap open as
MAGGIE says)

You're walking me out Sunday.

WILL

And you the master's daughter ... Well, by gum ...
(WILL's head descends as the
trap slowly closes.

MAGGIE sings:

MAGGIE   Piano Score No. 3B
(Sings)   Page 37

I WENT AND STOMPED MY FOOT ON THE FLOOR
THE WAY A CHILD WILL DO
WHEN UP THROUGH A DOOR A DOOR IN THE FLOOR
A MIRACLE CAME INTO VIEW

NOT A GLITTERING MIRACLE NOTHING SUBLIME
BUT THE TAWDRIEST MIRACLE COVERED WITH GRIME
AND HE DIDN'T SEEM MUCH LIKE THE PHRASES I'VE READ
WIPED HIS NOSE WITH HIS SLEEVE, AND "YOU STOMPED," HE SAID.

HE'S NOT SIR GALAHAD, BY A LOT
BUT IT STOMPED, AND HE'S THE GALAHAD I GOT.

(SHE goes into the house)

FADE OUT

The cellar of the bootery. A
workbench rises.

WILL and TUBBY are seated side by
  side as the workbench rises from
  the pit. THEY'RE both pounding
  lasts.

                    WILL
Tubby, did you hear what Miss Maggie said to me?

                    TUBBY
Aye ...

                    WILL
I don't know what I ought to do.

                    TUBBY
Well, she's the master's daughter. Better do what she
says ...

                    WILL
Aye.

          (MUSIC STARTS, WILL and TUBBY pound
          lasts same as above. WILL stops again)

                    WILL
Tubby, I've a question in mind to axe you ...

                    TUBBY
          (Points up)
About ... uh ... ?

                    WILL
Aye ... I mean, you be married to one on 'um ...

                    TUBBY
Aye ...

                    WILL
Well, what do you ... oh ... ?

                    TUBBY
Well, what do you what ... ?

                    WILL
What do you ... like ... well, what do you say to them?

                         TUBBY
No problem there, my lad. No problem there ...

              (TUBBY and WILL sing: "HOW
              D'YA TALK TO A GIRL?"

         "HOW D'YA TALK TO A GIRL?"   Piano Score No. 4
                                             Page 40

                         TUBBY
              (Sings)
HOW D'YA TALK TO A GIRL?
YA JUST LISTEN! YA JUST LISTEN! YA JUST LISTEN!
TO WHAT SHE HAS TO SAY!
YA LISTEN AND LISTEN AND LISTEN AND

HOW D'YA TALK TO A GIRL?
YA JUST STAND THERE, HAT'N HAND THERE
AND YOU LISTEN
WHILE SHE TALKS AWAY

EV'RY LITTLE WHILE
YA SMILE
'CEPT FOR NOW AND THEN
WHEN YA SMILE AGAIN!
SHE'LL THINK YOU'RE A CHARMER

HOW D'YA TALK TO A GIRL?
YA JUST LISTEN! YA JUST LISTEN!
AND THEN ONE DAY THE GIRL'S YOUR WIFE
AND YA LISTEN, YA LISTEN, YA LISTEN
THE REST OF YOUR LIFE!
YOUR NATURAL LIFE!
              (Spoken)
Is that clear?

                         WILL
Sort of ...

                         TUBBY
There's not all that much to it, you know.

                         WILL
Aye ...

                         TUBBY
              (Sings)
HOW D'YA TALK

                         WILL
HOW D'YA TALK

                         TUBBY
TO A GIRL?

                         — 23 —

                                    WILL
TO A GIRL?

                                    TUBBY
YA JUST LISTEN!

                                    WILL
YA JUST LISTEN!

                                    TUBBY
YA JUST LISTEN!

                                    WILL
YA JUST LISTEN!

                                    TUBBY
YA JUST LISTEN!

                                    WILL
YA JUST LISTEN!

                                    BOTH
TO WHAT IS ON HER MIND
YA LISTEN AND LISTEN AND LISTEN AND

                                    TUBBY
HOW D'YA SPEAK

                                    WILL
HOW D'YA SPEAK

                                    TUBBY
TO A GIRL?

                                    WILL
TO A GIRL?

                                    TUBBY
YA SAY LIDDLE

                                    WILL
YA SAY LIDDLE

                                    TUBBY
YOUR THUMBS TWIDDLE

                                    WILL
YOUR THUMBS TWIDDLE

                                    TUBBY
AND YOU LISTEN

                                    WILL
AND YOU LISTEN

BOTH
WHILE SHE TALKS YA BLIND!

TUBBY
IF SHE THINKS IT'S ODD

WILL
IF SHE THINKS IT'S ODD

TUBBY
YA NOD!

WILL
YA NOD!

TUBBY
NOT TO BE A BORE

WILL
NOT TO BE A BORE

TUBBY
YA JUST NOD ONCE MORE!

WILL
            (Spoken)
Once more?

TUBBY
SHE WILL THINK YOU'RE BRILLYANT!

WILL
            (HE's got it)
HOW D'YA TALK

TUBBY
            (Approvingly)
HOW D'YA TALK

WILL
TO A GIRL?

TUBBY
TO A GIRL?

WILL
YA JUST LISTEN!

TUBBY
YA JUST LISTEN!

WILL
YA JUST LISTEN!

                         TUBBY
YA JUST LISTEN!

                         WILL
AND THEN ONE DAY

                         TUBBY
AND THEN ONE DAY

                         BOTH
THE GIRL'S YOUR WIFE!
AND YA LISTEN, YA LISTEN, YA LISTEN
THE REST OF YOUR

YA LISTEN, YA LISTEN, YA LISTEN
THE REST OF YOUR

YA LISTEN, YA LISTEN, YA LISTEN
THE REST OF YOUR LIFE
YOUR NATURAL LI-I-IFE!

                    FAST FADE

The Moonrakers. The scene opens
with the millhands doing a CLOG
DANCE. After number, HOBSON
is seen at a downstage table with
HEELER. BEENSTOCK is outside the
door, passing out tracts and
buttonholing anyone who will
listen to him.

HEELER

Just look at him out there, Henry. You have to say one
thing for Beenstock, he doesn't give up. I thought after
last night he'd never show his face around here again.

HOBSON

It's a crime the way that man neglects his business ...

HEELER

Aye, but he's richer than the four of us put together.
Maybe you should try neglecting your business the same
way.

HOBSON

Gentlemen, enough of Beenstock. I want your opinion about
something, and I want it honest. You've been exposed
daily to the direction of my thinking and the sound of
my voice ...

HEELER

Aye, Henry, you're a fine talker, and that's a fact.

TUDSBURY   DENTON

Aye ...   That's right.

HOBSON

Then would you believe it, my friends, that in the eyes of
my daughters, I am a windbag?

TUDSBURY   DENTON   HEELER

No.   I don't believe it.   That can't be.

HOBSON

They scorn my wisdom and they badger me, day and night --
so, I've made a decision. The two youngest have got to go.
Now, I'm hoping you gentlemen will know some candidates to
take over the feeing and housing of those two females.

DENTON

Henry, you might not like this, but maybe your answer is standing right outside that door ...

HOBSON

What do you mean?

DENTON

Well, you must know Beenstock's boys have an eye for your two girls ...

HOBSON

I don't believe it!

HEELER

He's right, Henry. It's all over Salford ...

HOBSON

Oh, is it? Well, I'll soon put a stop to that.

HEELER

Now, don't be hasty, Henry. He's got two substantial boys.

HOBSON

I despise that man on principle ...

HEELER

One of them is reading the law and the other one is certain to take over the business ...

HOBSON

I said I despise that man on principle ...

DENTON

But, Henry, quick as a wink, your burden would become his ...

HOBSON

(Weighing it)
I never thought of it quite like that.

TUDSBURY

There's profit in it for you, Henry ...

HOBSON

Ay ... Oh no, no.
(Pulling himself together)
But there's a principle involved ...

HEELER

Henry, think of the advantage to you ...

HOBSON

I am ... I am.

                         DENTON
May, but it's out of the question.

                         HOBSON
And why may I ask?

                         DENTON
Beenstock'll want better than a drunken sot like you for
his family.

                         HOBSON
A drunken sot, is it?

                         HEELER
Aye ... it'd take a miracle to win him over.

                         HOBSON
A miracle, would it? Well, gentlemen, you are about to
witness one ... Beenstock ...

          (HOBSON rises and crosses to the
          door and opens it)

Beenstock, could I have a word with you?
          (HE comes downstage again)

                         HEELER
What about those principles, Henry?

                         HOBSON
I'll tell you my strongest principle ... Never let your
principles stand in the way of your profits.

          (BEENSTOCK is in and HE joins
          HOBSON downstage)

                         BEENSTOCK
What is it, Hobson?

                         HOBSON
Come over here for a minute. Beenstock, this is hard for
me to admit. But ... nay you wouldn't believe me, anyway
...

                         BEENSTOCK
Hobson, why not try me?

                         HOBSON
Well, those words you used last night ... the clarity and
feeling with which you spoke ... I am moving towards
temperance ...

BEENSTOCK

Hobson, I've always felt that deep ... very, very deep within you ... there's the trace of a decent man ... in spite of the fact that you always act like a damn fool ...

HOBSON

Thank you very much.

BEENSTOCK

So you've decided to wear the Blue Rosette, have you?

HOBSON

Nay, I haven't come quite that far. As I said, I'm moving toward temperance. Very, very slowly, mind you, but moving. Now as for wearing the Blue Rosette, I couldn't do that until I could be certain I could keep the pledge. After all, my word is as good as my bond.

BEENSTOCK

That's honest of you, Hobson, and I respect you for it.

HOBSON

However, I want one thing clear.

BEENSTOCK

What's that?

HOBSON

Don't think that because I'm moving in your direction on the issue of drink, that I've changed my mind about the love your boys have for my girls ...

BEENSTOCK

Oh, you know about that, too, ...

HOBSON

Aye ... I've known about it for quite a while. I think it time we both put a stop to it.

BEENSTOCK

Well, I'm none in favor of it either, for that matter.

HOBSON

Good. That's settled. And I know we're both strong enough to endure the criticism that'll fall on us ...

BEENSTOCK

Criticism, Hobson?

HOBSON

Criticism from those who sing of the glory of young love and the shame of blighting it in the bud.

                    BEENSTOCK
Well, I'm used to being criticized ...

                    HOBSON
And being called inhuman?

                    BEENSTOCK
Inhuman?

                    HOBSON
Aye, inhuman, for standing in the way of natural affection
between man and woman ...

                    BEENSTOCK
Hmmm ... maybe there is something to that point of view.

                    HOBSON
Nay, Beenstock. We'll stick to our guns even if it means
life-long misery for the four young people.

                    BEENSTOCK
But, Henry ...

                    HOBSON
Don't argue with me. My mind's made up ...

                    BEENSTOCK
Aye, but it was made up about drink ...

                    HOBSON
There you go, with your silver tongue ...

                    BEENSTOCK
Perhaps, we should, at least, consider ...

                    HOBSON
          (In fast)
You've gotten to me again. You're a magician ...

                    BEENSTOCK
Not really. It's just common sense ...

                    HOBSON
Exactly! You've convinced me. You've made yourself a deal.
          (Grabs his hand)

                    BEENSTOCK
I have ... ?

                    HOBSON
My girls and your boys!

                    BEENSTOCK
              (All too fast for him)
My boys and your girls ... ?

                    HOBSON
Done ... ?

                    BEENSTOCK
              (Faintly)
Done ...

                    TUDSBURY
Henry, you're a card.

                                        Piano Score No. 5B
                                        Page 68

            (FADE as HOBSON exits)

The Park. WILL and MAGGIE on
the bench.

MAGGIE

Will, we've been together the better part of the afternoon
and you've hardly said a word.

WILL

I've been devoting my time to just listening ...

MAGGIE

Well, it's time you spoke ...

WILL

Aye, if I must ...

MAGGIE

Well ...

WILL

By Gum, it's an awkward business, is this, Miss Maggie.

MAGGIE

What's awkward about it, lad?

WILL

There be just one thing as worries me in my head ...

MAGGIE

What's that?

WILL

Oh ...

MAGGIE

Come along, lad, out with it.

WILL

Although I've got great respect for you, Miss Maggie, I'm
bound to tell you that when it comes to marriage, I'm
none in love with thee.

MAGGIE

Wait till you're asked.
        (Pause)
Will, I want your hand in mind and your word that you'll g
through life with me for the best we can get out of it.

                              WILL
We'd not get much without there's love between us, Miss
Maggie.

                              MAGGIE
That'll come.

                              WILL
Suppose it doesn't?

                              MAGGIE
Then we'll get along without. I'm tired of watching the
years go by, every day the same ...

                              WILL
You're desperate set on courting me, Miss Maggie. What
would your father say?

                              MAGGIE
He'll say quite a lot, and it'll make no difference to me.

                              WILL
Much better not to upset him though.

                              MAGGIE
I'll be the judge of that. Salford life is too close to
the bone to see my best chance slip away from me through
fear of speaking out.

               (MUSIC STARTS)

                              WILL
I'm your best chance?

                              MAGGIE
Your are that.

                              WILL
Well, by gum ...

               (WILL sings: BEST CHANCE)   Piano Score No. 6
                                                 Page 69

               "IF I BE YOUR BEST CHANCE"

CHORUS:

IF I BE, BE YOUR BEST CHANCE
IF I BE YOUR BEST CHANCE OF ALL
IF I BE YOUR BEST CHANCE
THEN YOUR CHANCES AT BEST -- BE SMALL!

IF IF BE, BE YOUR ONE HOPE
IF I BE THE ONE HOPE YOU FOUND
IF I BE YOUR ONE HOPE
THERE'S A SCARCENESS OF HOPE --   AROUND!

                         - 34 -

WILL (Continued)

IF I BE NEAR TO BEING, WHAT YOU'RE SEEING AS A PRIZE
EITHER YOUR MIND IS FLEEING, OR YOU NEED SOME GLASSES
FOR THOSE BIG BROWN EY-EYES --

IF I BE, BE YOUR BEST CHANCE
IF IT'S ME THAT YOU'RE CHOOSING FIRST
IF I BE YOUR BEST CHANCE
I WOULD SURE HATE TO MEET -- YOUR WORST!!!

INTERLUDE:

WHEN I HEARD THAT STOMP
I KNEW THAT STOMP
WAS A STOMP I SHOULD IGNORE

BUT BEFORE I KNEW
WHAT BEST TO DO
I WAS WAIST HIGH IN THE STORE

I FELT NOT AT EASE
AND WEAK IN THE KNEES
WITH YOU TOW'RING LIKE A TREE

AND TRY AS I TRY
THERE'S NO WAY THAT I
SEE YOU WITH THE LIKES OF ME!!!

MAGGIE
(Speaks)
Stop under-estimating yourself Will Mossop, and right now.

WILL

IN MY SUNDAY BEST,
WITH TROUSERS PRESS'D
I'M DRESSED RIGHT TO THE TEETH
OH! I MAY LOOK GRAND
BUT UNDERSTAND
I'M WILL MOSSOP UNDERNEATH!!!

WHAT WOULD IT MEAN
WITH NO LOVE BETWEEN
OH IT RAISES AN AWESOME DOUBT

YOU BE SINCERE
BUT THE FEAR I FEAR
IS WE WOULDN'T HAVE MUCH WITHOUT --

MAGGIE
(Speaks)
You're still my best chance, Will.

                                   WILL
                 (Sings)
IF I BE, BE YOUR BEST CHANCE
IF IT'S ME YOU PICKED FOR YOUR GROOM
IF I BE YOUR BEST CHANCE
THEN I'M BOUNDED TO SAY,

                 (MUSIC echoes as HE starts to leave)

WALKING AWAY

                 (MUSIC echoes as HE pauses and
                 looks back)

IT'S BEEN A DAY,
BY GUM!!!
                 (HE leans on portal.

                 After song)

                                   MAGGIE
Will Mossop come here. I'll have your answer, now.

                                   WILL
But you know my answer ...

                                   MAGGIE
Good. Then you're going to marry me.

                                   WILL
Oh, nay ... I'm not really. I can't do that, Miss Maggie.
I can see I'm disturbing your arrangements like ... but
I'd be obliged if you would put this notion from you.

                                   MAGGIE
When I make arrangements, they're not for upsetting ...

                                   WILL
There's summat you should know, Miss Maggie ...

                                   MAGGIE
Now, listen to me, Will Mossop ...

                                   WILL
But it has great bearing ...

                                   MAGGIE
... the decision's been made. The banns will be posted
next Sunday ...

                                   WILL
Aye, that's the point. There'll be banns posted next
Sunday all right, but for me and Ada Figgens.

                                 — 36 —

MAGGIE

You and Ada Figgens?

WILL

Aye.

MAGGIE

Why didn't you say something?

WILL

I tried to, but you kept on cutting in ...

MAGGIE

Who's Ada Figgens?

WILL

The daughter where I lodge.

MAGGIE

That sandy-haired girl who brings you your dinner?

WILL

She's golden-haired is Ada.

MAGGIE

Aye, I know the breed. She's the helpless sort.

WILL

She does need protecting.

MAGGIE

I'll tell you this, my lad, it's a desperate poor kind a
woman who'll look for protection to the likes of you ...

(Open change to next scene   Piano Score No. 6A
as dialogue continues)   Page 82

Exterior. Street. Poor section
of Salford. ADA FIGGINS is sitting on the stoop of one of the
houses.

MAGGIE
(Turns and looks at ADA)
Just look at her. Born to meekness.
(Starts across)
I'll clip her wings and fast.
(To ADA)
Young woman, you're treading on my foot.

ADA
Me, Miss 'Obson?

WILL
Ada, she's wanting to put a stop ...

MAGGIE
You hold your hush. This is for me and her to settle.
Take a fair look at him, Ada.

ADA
At Will?

MAGGIE
Not much for two women to fall out over, is there?

ADA
I see the lad I'm going to wed.

MAGGIE
It's a funny thing, but I could say the same.

ADA
You!

WILL
Ada, that's what I've been trying to tell you, and by
gum, she'll have me from you if you don't be careful.

ADA
You're too late, Miss Hobson. Will and me is promised.

MAGGIE
That's the past. It's the future I'm looking to. What
idea have you for that? If it's a likelier one than mine,
you can have the lad.

ADA

I'm trusting him to make the future right.

MAGGIE

It's as bad as I thought. Will Mossop, you'll wed me.

ADA

Beggin' your pardon, Miss 'Obson, but you really shouldn't be doing this.

WILL

Aren't you going to put up a better fight for me than that, Ada? You're fair giving me to her.

ADA

I'm going to fetch my mother. Will Mossop, you'll have a thick ear to remember this day.
          (ADA goes into house)

MAGGIE

So it's her mother who's pushing this match?

WILL

She has her heart set on it ...

MAGGIE

I have no mother, Will.

WILL

You don't need one, either.

MAGGIE

Now listen to me, Will Mossop, you're to go inside and pack your things. I'll go along to Tubby's and see if he can put you up. We'll meet by the bench in park.

WILL

But, Mrs. Figgins has a terrible rough side to her nature.

MAGGIE

Are you afraid, Will?

WILL

Aye, I am that.

MAGGIE

It's a bad habit, but I'll help you overcome it.
          (MAGGIE starts off)

WILL

If I don't meet you, you'll know I've had a serious accident.

(MAGGIE looks at him)

                    MAGGIE
You'll meet me.
          (MAGGIE goes)

Piano Score No. 6B
Page 83

                    WILL
Aye, and if I do meet you, I'm afraid I'll have one,
too ...
          (WILL starts into the house. As
          HE nears the door, HE loses his
          nerve and turns and comes down the
          steps. MRS. FIGGINS appears in the
          doorway, followed by ADA)

                    MRS. FIGGINS
Well, look who's 'ere ...

                    WILL
          (Turns)
Oh, hello, Mrs. Figgins.

                    MRS. FIGGINS
What's new, Willie ... ?

                    WILL
Oh, nothing ... nothing, much ..

                    MRS. FIGGINS
What's this my Ada tells me about you and Miss ... Miss
'Obson?

                    WILL
Oh, that ... Just a bit of idle gossip, Mrs. Figgins.

                    MRS. FIGGINS
I'm glad to hear that, Willie. You know it's filled me
with joy the way you and my Ada have taken to each other.

                    WILL
Aye, it's a joyful thing ...

                    MRS. FIGGINS
You're joyful about it, too, are you?

                    WILL
Very joyful.

                    MRS. FIGGINS
You don't look joyful ...

                    WILL
I'm not much at showing my feelings ...

                    - 40 -

MRS. FIGGINS

Well, you better start showing them, Willie ...

WILL

Aye, I suppose I better had.
          (WILL retreats as two men
          advance towards him but ends up
          squarely against MRS. FIGGINS)

MRS. FIGGINS

Come on lad, be joyful.

          (WILL   dances)

MRS. FIGGINS

Joyfuller.   Piano Score No. 7
                                                    Page 88
          (HE dances again)
Come on, Willie, you can do better than that.
          (SHE pushes him forward and the
          barrel dance begins)

          (Dance ends, but resumes as MAGGIE
          enters and interrupts)

MAGGIE

Stop it!

          (EVERYONE stops what THEY are
          doing)

That'll be enough of that!

ADA

That's her, Mum ... that's Miss 'Obson ...

MAGGIE

And if you don't want the Salford police on your necks,
you and your friends will take your hands from Will
Mossop.
          (SHE turns on the group)
I mean it ... I'll remember your faces and have you all
hauled into police court, every last one of you.
          (To WILL)
Go get your things, Will.

          (WILL goes into the house)

MRS. FIGGINS
          (Coming to MAGGIE
Now, look here, Miss 'Obson, why don't you go back to
Chapel Street and stay out of where you don't belong ...

                    MAGGIE
When I leave, Will leaves with me.

                    ADA
I told you, Mum.

                    MRS. FIGGINS
Will aint goin nowhere. He's going to marry Ada and
settle down right here.

                    MAGGIE
And be an eighteen-shilling-a-week boothand for the rest
cf his life? Will Mossop's an artist.

                    MRS. FIGGINS
Will Mossop?

          (WILL re-enters from house
          carrying a suitcase)

                    MAGGIE
Aye. He has the feel of leather in his hands. He can
shape it, cut it, and saw it better than any man I've
ever seen at bench. It's a genius, and I won't see
it wasted. He's going to marry me, Mrs. Figgins, and
I'm going to see that he becomes the finest bootmaker
in all of Lancashire and wins the respect he's entitled
to.

                    MRS. FIGGINS
Miss 'Obson, I don't understand half what you're saying
...

                    MAGGIE
I know that, Mrs. Figgins, but one day when you see Will
Mossop's name up on a shop, you'll understand that he
did the right thing by leaving here.

                    MRS. FIGGINS
Now, hold on ...

                    MAGGIE
          (To WILL)
Come along, Will. There won't be any more trouble
here ...

          (WILL picks up his bag apprehensively
          and follows MAGGIE out)

                    ADA
Mum, it's daylight robbery ...

MRS. FIGGINS
(Pushing ADA into the house)
That woman certainly gives you your ear's worth.
(Goes to steps of house)
I wonder what she'd charge to do m' funeral.

(SHE goes)

Piano Score No. 7A
Page 108

An alley, lit by one gaslight.
Evening of the same day.

After a moment MAGGIE moves in
and under the light. SHE looks
back into the darkness.

MAGGIE

Will ... ? Willie ... ?

(WILL enters and comes into
the light)

WILL

Aye ...

MAGGIE

What's taking you so long?

WILL

It's slow moving away from what you know into summat
you don't.

MAGGIE

You're finished staying there.

WILL

And I've not to go back there, never no more?

MAGGIE

Nay. You're not.

WILL

It's hard to believe ... You do arrange things, Miss Maggie.

MAGGIE

You'll stay at Tubby's.

WILL

At Tubby's?

MAGGIE

Aye ... But not for long. We'll post banns right away.
In three weeks we'll be married.

(WILL reacts with alarm)

Now ... you can kiss me, Will.

— 44 —

                        WILL
Well, that's forcing things a bit and all, Miss Maggie ...

                        MAGGIE
It may be some time before we get another chance ...

                        WILL
But right here ... in public street ...

                        MAGGIE
Aye ...

                        WILL
But it's like saying I agree to everything ... a kiss is ...

                        MAGGIE
Oh, come along, lad, get it over ...

              (HE approaches her, but backs
              off at the last moment)

                        WILL
Nay, I couldn't ...

                        MAGGIE
Very well, lad. I can see you can't take too much at one
swallow. Now, you'd best get over to Tubby's and make
sure of your bed ...

                        WILL
Yes, Miss Maggie ...

              (SHE starts off, then turns back)

                        MAGGIE
Don't be long.

                        WILL
No, Miss Maggie ...

                        MAGGIE
After Tubby's come right to shop.

                        WILL
Yes, Miss Maggie.

                        MAGGIE
The night's not over yet ...

                        WILL
No, Miss Maggie.

              (SHE goes.

                              WILL (Continued)
I didn't expect it would be ...
          (WILL Sings:)

YES! MISS MAGGIE, NO! MISS MAGGIE   Piano Score No. ?
SHALL I STAY OR GO? MISS MAGGIE   Page 109
TAKE MISS MAGGIE? PUT MISS MAGGIE?
SHALL I KISS YOUR FOOT? MISS MAGGIE?

OUR PARTNERSHIP IS CLEARLY ON CONDITION
THAT I'M THE ONE WHO BOWS TO YOUR AMBITION
I'M SCARED TO DEATH, TO TAKE A BREATH,
UNLESS I'VE GOT YOUR MAJESTY'S PERMISSION

WELL, YOU CAN'T MAKE ME SQUIRM,
          (Shouts off)   MISS MAGGIE!
WILL MOSSOP'S NOT A WORM,
          (Shouts louder)   MISS MAGGIE!

          (MAGGIE re-enters)

                         MAGGIE
Did you call, Will?

                         WILL
          (Speaks ... all innocence)
Me? Call you, Miss Maggie? No.

                         MAGGIE
Don't dawdle, there's still much to do!
          (SHE goes)

                         WILL   Piano Score No. 9
VERSE   Page 111

I NEVER HAVE QUESTIONED THE WAY OF THINGS
I TOOK THE GOOD WITH THE BAD
WHEN LIFE DIDN'T SERVE ME A TRAY OF THINGS
I MADE DO WITH THE TRAY I HAD, --

BUT YOU'VE GOT TO HAVE AN ANSWER
WHEN THE QUESTION IS KISSING
ESPECIALLY WHEN YOU FEEL
THERE'S SOMETHING MISSING

CHORUS

WHAT MAKES IT HAPPEN
WHAT BRINGS THE WONDER
WHAT STARTS THE THUNDER
YOU HEAR IN YOUR HEART

WHAT MAKES THE MAGIC
THAT MAKES LIFE WORTH WHILE
KEEPS YOU ON EARTH WHILE
YOU'RE SOMEWHERE APART

ONE DAY YOU'RE NOTHING
NEXT DAY YOU'RE SOMETHING
BECAUSE OF SOMEONE YOU HAPPEN TO SEE

WHAT MAKES IT HAPPEN
WHAT MAKES LOVE HAPPEN
WHEN WILL IT HAPPEN TO ME??

INTERLUDE

WHAT MAKES IT HAPPEN
WHAT MAKES LOVE HAPPEN
WHEN WILL IT HAPPEN TO ME
OH, WHEN WILL IT HAPPEN TO ME ???

The bootery. In complete darkness

                    HOBSON (Off)
          (Shouting)
Where are they? I want to get my hands on those two scoun-
drels. Just give me a few mintues with them I'll change
their tune!
                    (HOBSON storms in through the house
                    door, HE is holding a paper in one
                    hand. Light floods the shop through
                    the door.

                    VICKIE and ALICE follow him into
                    the shop)

                    VICKIE
I told you they'd gone, Father, ... please compose yourself ...

                    HOBSON
          (Exploding)
It's a plot against the middle class.

                    ALICE
          (Perplexed)
What's the matter, father?

                    (ALICE guides HOBSON to a chair)

                    HOBSON
Have you any idea what this is?

                    VICKIE
Well, of course, it's the marriage contract.

                    ALICE
Your slippers, father ...

                    HOBSON
          (Sits, waving the paper)
Have you any idea what it says ... ?

                    (ALICE kneels before him putting
                    on his slippers)

                    ALICE
Albert drew it up himself.

HOBSON

Aye. I believe it. It's a typical lawyer's piece of
thievery ...

VICKIE

Thievery, father?

HOBSON

Five hundred pounds worth! It's here in black and white!
The undersigned agrees to pay the sum of five hundred
pounds as marriage settlements for his daughters, this
sum to be transferred in two drafts of two hundred and
fifty pounds each ... ! The undersigned is me, only
there won't be any undersigned ...

VICKIE

You can afford it, father.

HOBSON

Afford is one thing, paying is another ...

ALICE

But you've got to bait your hook to catch fish ...

VICKIE

Especially temperance fish ...

HOBSON
          (Stands)
Then I'll none go fishing ...
          (HE tears up the paper)
That's what I think of your Albert's handiwork. There'll
be no settlements and no marriages ...

ALICE

But we've told everyone ...

VICKIE

You'll come out looking cheap, Father.

HOBSON

I can stand that easier than parting with five hundred
pounds. I should have known better than to trust that
abstemious ass ... All the time I thought I was doing it
to him, he was doing it to me ...
          (HE goes)

VICKIE

It is a bit much ... five hundred pounds. Your Albert
shows a grasping hand in that ...

ALICE

My Albert? I see Freddie's head for trade in that sum.

VICKIE

Freddie's not in trade. He's in wholesale. And your
Albert admitted drawing up the paper ...

(MAGGIE enters the street door)

MAGGIE

Eee! What's the matter with you two?

VICKIE	ALICE
Oh, nothing. Our weddings	Oh, Nothing ...
are off, that's all ...	

MAGGIE

Oh no. I thought Father and Mr. Beenstock had come to
terms ...

ALICE

Except for one small detail ...

MAGGIE

The settlements ... that's it, isn't it?

VICKIE

Five hundred pounds ...

ALICE

And Father won't pay a shilling.

MAGGIE

Well, there's no use sitting around arguing about whose
fault it is, is there.

VICKIE

What can we do?

MAGGIE

Well, I want one thing straight from you two. Do you
really want your Freddie ... and do you really want your
Albert?

ALICE	VICKIE
Oh, yes, Maggie.	More than anything ...

MAGGIE

Then it's worth putting our minds to it ...   Piano Score No. 10
    (Wood block tic)   Page 120

VICKIE

Maggie, do you have an idea ...

ALICE

Please tell us.

                              MAGGIE
Oh, nothing yet.

                              VICKIE
Oh, Maggie, please help us.

                              ALICE
Please.

                              MAGGIE
Oh nothing's hopeless, luv, if you put your mind to it.

          (Tics)

A thinking mind can solve any problem.
          (MAGGIE, joined by ALICE and VICKIE
          sing: USE YOUR NOGGIN)

          "USE YOUR NOGGIN"
                              MAGGIE
          (Sings)
VERSE

YOU'VE GOT TO JUST USE YOUR NOGGIN

                              GIRLS
JUST USE YOUR NOGGIN

                              MAGGIE
YOU'VE GOT TO JUST USE YOUR BEAN

                              VICKIE
USE YOUR BEAN

                              ALICE
USE YOUR BEAN

                              MAGGIE
YOU'VE GOT TWO EARS ON YOUR FACE
AND ALL OF THAT SPACE -- THAT SPACE IN BETWEEN

                              GIRLS
SPACE IN BETWEEN

                              MAGGIE
WHEN LIFE TREATS YOU POORLY IN PARTICULAR

                              GIRLS
IN PARTICULAR

                              MAGGIE
THAT'S WHEN YOU MUST HAVE FAITH AND TRUST, AND MORE THAN
JUST STAY PERPENDICULAR.

                    MAGGIE (Continued)
YOU'VE GOT TO JUST USE YOUR BONNET

                    GIRLS
JUST USE YOUR BONNET

                    MAGGIE
WHEN ALL YOUR HOPES START TO SINK

                    ALL
WHEN THE FUTURE'S GLOOMY AS A POT

                    MAGGIE
                              OF PRINTERS INK
YOU'LL FIND YOUR CARES WILL ALL TOBOGGAN

                    ALL
YOU'LL FIND YOUR CARES WILL ALL TOBOGGAN
YOU WILL SEND YOUR TROUBLES JOGGIN

                    GIRLS
YOU'LL FIND YOUR CARES WILL ALL TOBOGGAN

                    ALL
IF YOU'LL ONLY USE YOUR NOGGIN
AND THINK!

                    VICKIE
        (Spoken)
Do you have a solution yet, Maggie?

                    MAGGIE
Not yet, but let's keep thinking.

                    VICKIE & ALICE
        (Sing)
YOU'VE GOT TO JUST USE YOUR NOGGIN

                    MAGGIE
JUST USE YOUR NOGGIN

                    VICKIE & ALICE
YOU'VE GOT TO JUST USE YOUR BEAN

                    MAGGIE
YOUR BEAN

                    ALL
YOU'VE GOT TWO EARS ON YOUR FACE
AND ALL OF THAT SPACE -- THAT SPACE IN BETWEEN

                    MAGGIE
SET-BACKS CAN BE MADE INFINITESIMAL

                    - 52 -

                              ALL
NEXT TIME YOU ADD, IF THINGS LOOK BAD, DON'T BE TOO SAD
JUST MOVE THE DECIMAL

                         ALICE & VICKIE
YOU'VE GOT TO JUST USE YOUR BONNET
EACH TIME YOU COME TO THE BRINK

                              ALL
PROBLEMS ARE LIKE WOOLEN HOSE THEY'LL MORE THAN LIKELY
                                              SHRINK

YOU'LL FIND YOUR CARES WILL ALL TOBOGGAN
YOU WILL SEND YOUR TROUBLES JOGGIN
IF YOU'LL ONLY USE YOUR NOGGIN AND
ONLY USE YOUR NOGGIN AND
ONLY USE YOUR NOGGIN AND
THINK

                    (WILL enters exterior, and as the
                    song ends HE knocks on the door.
                    ALICE looks through the glass and
                    turns to MAGGIE in amazement)

                         ALICE
Maggie, it's Will Mossop.

                         MAGGIE
Well, let him come in.

                         ALICE
But he's neigh on twelve hours too early.

                    (MAGGIE crosses to the door and
                    opens it)

                         MAGGIE
Come on in, Will.

                    (WILL enters)

                         VICKIE
You're . bit early for work, aren't you?

                         WILL
For work? Aye, I'd say I'm a bit early ... for work.

                         MAGGIE
Will's come to talk to father.

                         WILL
I have ... ?

                         MAGGIE
Just out of respect, he's going to ask father for my hand.

                         WILL
I am ... ?   — 53 —

                    ALICE
              (Horrified)
You're going to marry Will Mossop?

                    VICKIE
              (Equally horrified)
Maggie, you can't ...

                    MAGGIE
Why, is there something wrong with him?

                    ALICE
He can't even read or write ...

                    WILL
Perhaps I'd best come back some other time ...

                    MAGGIE
You'll stay here, Will. I've decided to marry you, and it
appears that a lot of people are going to have to get used
to the idea.

              (The door from the house slams
              open. HOBSON enters, frowning)

                    HOBSON
Oh, for heaven's sake, Maggie, an end to this geese
cackling! Isn't a man entitled to a little peace on
the Lord's Day ... ?
              (HE looks at WILL puzzled)
Who's that?

                    MAGGIE
That's Will, Father.

                    HOBSON
Oh, go back home, Willie. You're a whole night too early.

                    WILL
Aye. Thank you very much, sir.
              (WILL starts for the door)

                    MAGGIE
Will, don't leave.

                    HOBSON
Why shouldn't he leave? What's going on here?

                    ALICE
              (As if WILL weren't there)
Father, what do you think of Will Mossop?

                    HOBSON
A decent lad. I've nowt against him ... that I know of.

                    VICKIE
How would you like him in the family?

                    HOBSON
In whose family?

                    MAGGIE
In our family, father. I'm going to marry Will Mossop.

                    HOBSON
Marry ... you ... Mossop ...

                    MAGGIE
Aye, you thought me past the marrying age. Well, I'm not.
I've chosen my man.

                    HOBSON
If there's any choosing of husbands to be done, I will do
the choosing ... And I don't choose him!

                    MAGGIE
You never intended choosing anybody! So I've done it
for myself!

                    HOBSON
Maggie, you can't have Will Mossop. I'd be the laughing
stock of the place if I allowed it. Why, he's a workhouse
brat. A come-by-chance.

                    MAGGIE
I am marrying Will Mossop, Father.

                    HOBSON
Maggie, don't talk like that ...
          (HE shudders)
... it's hardly decent at your time of life.

                    MAGGIE
You and I 'ull be straight with one another, father. I'm
not a fool and you're not a fool and things may as well
be put in their place as left untidy. So I'll state my
terms short and clear. You will pay my man, Will Mossop,
double his present wages. As for me, who's given you
years of work without wages, I'll work eight hours a day
in future and you'll pay me fifteen shillings by the week.

                    HOBSON
Do you think I'm made of brass?

                    MAGGIE
You'll soon be made of less than you are if you let Willie
go. That's what you've got to face.

HOBSON

I might face it, Maggie. Boothands are cheap.

MAGGIE

Aye, cheap ones are cheap. The sort you'd have to watch
all day, while all your friends are supping their ale without you. I'm value to you, so's my man; and you can boast
at the Moonrakers that your daughter Maggie's made the
strangest, finest match a woman's made this fifty year. Now,
you can put your hand in your pocket and do what I propose.

HOBSON

I'll show you what I propose.
            (Turns to WILL)
Will Mossop, step forward here.

MAGGIE

I've got my eye on you, my lad ...

        (WILL steps forward and faces
        HOBSON)

WILL

There's no need to get wrought up so, Mr. Hobson ...

HOBSON

No need?!

WILL

No!

HOBSON

When you've taken up with my Maggie behind my back?

WILL

Nay, I've not. She's done the taking up.

HOBSON
        (HE starts to unbuckle his
        wide belt)
Well, Willie, either way, love has led you astray. Mind you,
you can keep your job. I don't bear malice, but we must
beat the love from your body ...

WILL

You're making a great mistake, Mr. Hobson. There's no love
in me to beat. I'm not wanting thy Maggie. It's her that's
after me.

        (HOBSON snaps belt)
But touch me with that belt, and I'll take her quick, aye,
and I'll stick to her like glue.

                              HOBSON
There's no but one answer to that kind of talk, my lad.
                    (HOBSON takes the belt and hits
                    WILL across the chest. There is
                    a moment of silence as the two
                    men stare at each other)

                              WILL
And I've no but one answer to that, Mr. Hobson.
                    (HE turns to MAGGIE)
Miss Maggie, I've none kissed you yet. I shirked before.
But, by gum, I'll kiss you now.
                    (WILL kisses MAGGIE in anger at
                    HOBSON. HE then turns back to
                    HOBSON. HOBSON hits him again
                    with the belt. WILL turns and
                    kisses MAGGIE again. Then HE
                    turns back to HOBSON)
Raise that strap to me again, Mr. Hobson, and I'll be forced
to go further.
                    (WILL and HOBSON stare at each
                    other for another moment. then
                    HOBSON strikes again. WILL
                    turns to MAGGIE)
Right! Come on, Miss Maggie ...
                    (HE holds out his arm. MAGGIE
                    takes it and HE leads her to the
                    door)

                              HOBSON
Where do you think you're going?

                              WILL
                    (WILL turns back and faces HOBSON)
We're leaving, Mr. Hobson. We don't know exactly where
we're going, but, by gum, we'll find a place and set up in
business for ourselves.
                    (WLL opens the door and HE and
                    MAGGIE leave)

                              MAGGIE
Oh, Willie ...

                    (WILL collapses and faints dead away,
                    falling like a piece of lumber on
                    his back.

                    MAGGIE kneels and places his hat
                    under his head and brushes back
                    his hair)

                                                  Piano Score No. 11
              C U R T A I N   Page 128

                              — 57 —

Scene 1

MRS. HEPWORTH's sitting room.

At rise, the FOOTMAN enters followed
by MAGGIE and WILL.

FOOTMAN

Right this way, please. Mrs. Hepworth will be with you in
a moment.
          (Indicating chairs)
Sit here.
          (HE goes as MAGGIE and WILL seat
          themselves. WILL perches on the
          extreme edge of the chair, a bowler
          clutched in his hands)

WILL

Miss Maggie, has your father got a forgiving nature?

MAGGIE

Why do you ask that, Will?

WILL

I must have taken leave of my senses. If I were to go to
him and apologize do you think ...

MAGGIE

I'll have no more talk like that. Sit back. You don't
damage the chair ...

WILL

Aye ...
          (HE tries sitting back)

MAGGIE

Isn't that more comfortable?

WILL

          (Moving to the edge of the chair
          again)
It's more comfortable being uncomfortable. Miss Maggie,
you'd best do the talking ...

MAGGIE

It's your work she admires ...

WILL

Aye, but you have such a way with words.

                    MAGGIE
Words the come from the heart have wings, Will.

                         WILL
There you are, e'ya see? That's what I mean ...

          (MRS. HEPWORTH sweeps into the room.
          MAGGIE rises. WILL is too awed to
          move. Finally MAGGIE catches his
          eye and indicates the standing
          dowager. WILL remembers his instruc-
          tions and rises)

                    MRS. HEPWORTH
Good afternoon. I'm sorry to have kept you waiting.

                    MAGGIE
Oh, that's quite all right, Mrs. Hepworth.

                    MRS. HEPWORTH
I remember you from the shop, Miss Hobson ...
          (SHE concentrates her glance on WILL)
But you ... ? Have we met before?

                    WILL
Aye. We have that.

                    MAGGIE
It's Will. Also from the shop. From down below ...

          (MRS. HEPWORTH is not illuminated)

                    WILL
One of the rabbits ... ?

                    MRS. HEPWORTH
Oh, of course. The man that actually makes those wonderful
boots ...

                    WILL
          (Modestly)
Aye ...

                    MAGGIE
Mrs. Hepworth, Mr. Mossop has something he wishes to talk
to you about.

                    MRS. HEPWORTH
          (To WILL)
Mr. Mossop ... ?

                    WILL
Mr. Mossop ... ? Oh, aye.

                         — 59 —

                    MAGGIE
              (A little impatient)
Will, tell Mrs. Hepworth what you propose.

                    WILL
What I propose? Aye. Well, I know it's naught that would
interest you ... but Miss Hobson and I be planning to open
our own shop.

                    MRS. HEPWORTH
Oh.

                    WILL
Aye.

                    MRS. HEPWORTH
Really?

                    WILL
Mmmmm ...

                    MRS. HEPWORTH
Well, you have my best wishes. Just leave your new address.
When I need your services, I'll send my carriage.

                    WILL
Right. Thank you very much, Mrs. Hepworth.

                    MAGGIE
Will, there's more.

                    WILL
Aye. There's always more.

          (MRS. HEPWORTH stops, turns and
           crosses back to the chair)

                    MRS. HEPWORTH
What is this all about? Speak up, man, I haven't all day.
Well?

                    MAGGIE
Willie.

                    WILL
We've come to borrow some money.

                    MRS. HEPWORTH
Borrow some money?

                    WILL
Aye ... We'd like to borrow a hundred pounds to start a boot
business ... a business the future of which seems ...

          (MRS. HEPWORTH stares at him)
                    — 60 —

                    WILL (Continued)
... not very good.

                    MRS. HEPWORTH
Astonishing ...

                    WILL
Aye, that's the very word ...

                    MRS. HEPWORTH
Tell me, Mr. Mossop, how in the world could you inagine that
I'd ever invest a hundred pounds in trade ... ?

                    WILL
Oh, it were a flash of madness ...

                    MRS. HEPWORTH
It was indeed, Mr. Mossop ...

          (WILL sags)

I'm sure you can see how ludicrous the whole idea is ...

          (WILL sags even further)

The boot business ... oh, really!

          (WILL is now totally crushed)

                    MAGGIE
Mrs. Hepworth ...

                    MRS. HEPWORTH
Yes?

                    MAGGIE
Mr. Mossop is an extremely capable bootmaker, and I would
like to point out that an investment ...

                    MRS. HEPWORTH
Miss Hobson, I never questioned Mr. Mossop's ability as a
bootmaker. However, establishing a new shop in Salford is
quite another thing ...

                    WILL
But you did give me your card, Mrs. Hepworth, and Miss
Maggie said that you got plenty of money and wouldn't miss
a hundred pounds. But as I said to Miss Maggie, I said a
hundred pounds is a lot of money and she said, well, it
wouldn't matter because you had your money left to you and
never had to work for it like us ...

                    MAGGIE
Will ... would you wait outside for a moment ... ?

                    — 61 —

        (WILL leaves)

                    MRS. HEPWORTH
I don't think he'd quite finished.

                    MAGGIE
I'm sorry for all those things he said, Mrs. Hepworth.

                    MRS. HEPWORTH
That's quite all right, Miss Hobson.

                    MAGGIE
Mrs. Hepworth, Will Mossop and I are going to be married.

                    MRS. HEPWORTH
Really?

                    MAGGIE
Aye.

                    MRS. HEPWORTH
Well, I don't approve of marrying across class lines ...
but I suppose the world is changing ...

                    MAGGIE
Aye, it is. And a loan from you would mean the start of a
new life for both of us.

                    MRS. HEPWORTH
Miss Hobson, aren't you placing all your eggs in a rather
flimsy basket ... ?

                    MAGGIE
Perhaps. Perhaps.
        (MAGGIE sings: I'LL MAKE A MAN OF THE MAN)

        "I'LL MAKE A MAN OF THE MAN"   Piano Score No. 13
                                            Page 135
                    MAGGIE
            (Sings)
BUT I'LL MAKE A MAN OF THE MAN
ALTHOUGH HE'S NO DREAM
I'LL MAKE ALL I CAN OF THE MAN
THO' FOOLISH I'LL SEEM

I'LL TEACH HIM TO REACH FOR MY HAND
AND TO HELP WITH MY GLOVE
I'LL TEACH HIM TO SIGH WHENEVER I SIGH
TO LAUGH WHEN I LAUGH, TO CRY WHEN I CRY
AND MAYBE, PERHAPS, EVEN TO FALL IN LOVE

AND WHEN HE IS ALL OF THE THINGS
THAT I KNOW HE CAN BE
THEN MAYBE HE'LL MAKE A WOMAN OF ME

                    — 62 —

(MRS. HEPWORTH rises and crosses to
door, then stops and turns back to
MAGGIE)

MRS. HEPWORTH
Miss Hobson, you can count on my help.
(SHE leaves)

MAGGIE
(Sings)
MAYBE HE'LL MAKE A WOMAN OF ME

FADE OUT.   Piano Score No. 13A
                             Page 142

ACT II

Scene 2

> A cellar, below street level.
> Stairs leading down. Cartons,
> boxes, old pieces of furniture
> are strewn about. The walls are
> dirty. The whole place is dismal
> and in disrepair. A door leads
> into the bedroom.
>
> As the lights come up, TUDSBURY
> goes up the stairs.

TUDSBURY

A little imagination and some elbow grease and you've got
yourself one of the best locations in Salford ...

> (MAGGIE followed by WILL comes down
> the stairs. HE's carrying a sign)

I'll let you have it ... as a personal favor ... for fifteen
shillings, the week ... providing you clean it up your-
selves.

MAGGIE

Ten shillings ... and you'll have all your rubbish out of
here by tonight.

TUDSBURY

You heard my terms.

MAGGIE

Come along, Willie ... Will.

TUDSBURY

As a special favor ... because of my fondness for your
father ... twelve and six ...
> (Points to WILL)
And he gives me a hand clearing my things ...

MAGGIE

Ten and six, and he'll give you no hand, he has his own work
to do.

TUDSBURY
> (Undecided)
Well ... I don't know ...

MAGGIE
> (Pressing)
And I'll buy the cretonne from you to dress up the windows.

— 64 —

                    TUDSBURY
You will?

                    MAGGIE
Aye.

                    TUDSBURY
Done!

                    MAGGIE
... if ...
          (SHE has him)
... if you give us the use of your tip-cart for the day ...

                    TUDSBURY
          (Defeated)
It's in the blood. All right. One month in advance.

                    MAGGIE
Two pounds even, Will.

                    TUDSBURY
Two pounds even?! That's two shillings short.

                    MAGGIE
We'll take a discount for cash.

          (WILL opens a small bag and takes
          two pound coins from it and holds
          them up. TUDSBURY shrugs and takes
          the money)

                    TUDSBURY
          (Ruefully)
Thank you. I'll send my boy down later for my things.
          (HE goes.

     WILL looks at the sack)

                    MAGGIE
What are you staring at, Will?

                    WILL
Mrs. Hepworth's money. It seems downright sinful to be
spending it.

                    MAGGIE
Well, she lent it to us to be spent. And there'll be a lot
more gone out of that sack by the time we open for business
tomorrow morning.

                    WILL
          (In disbelief)
Tomorrow morning?! But I can't get all this cleared up by
tomorrow morning.

                         MAGGIE
                (SHE takes out a slip of paper and
                hands it to WILL)
Here's a list of things we need. Take Tudsbury's cart and
start at the Flat Iron market. I'll go over every inch
here with soap and water.

                         WILL
                (Staring at the list)
But who's to set the prices on these things? Who's to do
the bargaining?

                         MAGGIE
You are, lad.

                         WILL
But I've no experience at such things.

                         MAGGIE
There'll be a lot of business things you'll have to do about
which you've had no experience. This is a partnership,
Will. You'll have to pull your weight.

                         WILL
Don't you worry about me, Miss Maggie. I intend to do my
share.

                         MAGGIE
Willie, I know that ...

                (HE starts off. MAGGIE looks at the
                sign)

Would you hang that on your way out ... ?

                         WILL
Aye ...
                (WILL walks heavily to the sign,
                picks it up and moves slowly toward
                the door)

                         MAGGIE
Willie, I don't like the way you're putting one foot in
front of t'other ...

                         WILL
                (Puzzled)
You don't ... ?

                         MAGGIE
No. That's the walk of a sad man ... a man afraid of life.
You're not that, Will.

                         — 66 —

                                WILL
But I've only got two feet, Miss Maggie. I don't see what
difference it makes how I use 'em.

                    (MAGGIE sings: "WALKING HAPPY")

          "WALKING HAPPY"   Piano Score No. 14
                                             Page 143

                                MAGGIE
               (Sings)
VERSE:

YOU CAN TELL 'BOUT THE MANNER OF A MAN BY THE SHAPE OF HIS
     HEAD
IT HAS BEEN SAID.

                                WILL
               (Speaks)
You can?

                                MAGGIE
               (Sings)
YOU CAN TELL IF HIS CHARACTER IS FINE BY A LINE IN HIS HAND
I UNDERSTAND

                                WILL
               (Speaks)
His hand?

                                MAGGIE
               (Sings)
BUT MY OWN METHOD FOR JUDGING PEOPLE I MEET
IS BY THE WAY THEY USE
THE SHOES ON THEIR FEET!

CHORUS:

THERE'S THE KIND OF WALK YOU WALK
WHEN THE WORLD'S UNDONE YOU
THERE'S THE KIND OF WALK YOU WALK
WHEN YOU'RE WALKIN' PROUD

THERE'S THE KIND OF WALK YOU WALK
WHEN THE NEIGHBORS SHUN YOU
THERE'S THE KIND OF WALK YOU WALK
SETS YOU 'BOVE THE CROWD.

                                WILL
               (Interrupts, but MUSIC under)
I appreciate the advice, Miss Maggie. There appears to be
much about me that needs changing ...

                                MAGGIE
Nay, Willie, I didn't mean ...

                              - 67 -

MAGGIE (Continued)
          (Stops, then continues)
Yes, as a matter of fact there is ...

                    WILL
I don't know if I'll ever be able to come up to your
measure ...

                    MAGGIE
But you can try, my lad. Now, step out of here with the
walk of the Will-Mossop-to-be.

          (WILL tries to pull himself to full
          height and walks awkwardly. HE
          abandons the effort self-consciously
          and goes through the door to the
          exterior. MAGGIE exits. The lights
          fade on the interior as WILL hangs
          up the sign. HE starts to walk away,
          when suddenly HE stops, turns and
          looks at sign)

                                        Piano Score No. 14A
                    WILL   Page 149
William Mossop, Master Bootmaker. Well, by gum.

          (Sings)
THERE'S THE KIND OF WALK YOU WALK
WHEN YOU FEEL LIKE CROWING
THERE'S THE KIND OF WALK YOU WALK
WHEN YOU'RE ON YOUR WAY

THERE'S THE KIND OF WALK YOU WALK
WHEN YOUR PRIDE IS SHOWING
AND THE KIND OF WALK YOU WALK
WHEN TODAY'S YOUR DAY

THERE'S THE KIND OF WALK YOU WALK
WHEN THE WORLD'S ALL RAINBOWS
AND YOUR HEART'S HOPPIN' LIKE A POPINJAY

GOOD FORTUNE'S FOUND YOU CHAPPIE
AND YOUR LIFE'S A HAPPY VALENTINE
WHEN YOU'RE WALKING HAPPY
DON'T THE BLOOMING WORLD SEEM FINE!!!

          (WILL dances)

GOOD FORTUNE'S FOUND YOU CHAPPIE
AND YOUR LIFE'S A HAPPY VALENTINE
WHEN YOU'RE WALKING HAPPY
DON'T THE BLOOMIN' WORLD SEEM FINE!!!

                    — 68 —

ACT II

Scene 3

Flat Iron Market.

Piano Score No. 14B
Page 155

ALL

THERE'S THE KIND OF WALK YOU WALK
WHEN YOU'RE FEELING AMPLE
THERE'S THE KIND OF WALK YOU WALK
WHEN YOU'RE FEELING LOW

THERE'S THE KIND OF WALK YOU WALK
SETS A FINE EXAMPLE
LIKE THE WALK YOU TAKE TO CHURCH
FOR THAT SUNDAY GLOW

THERE'S THE KIND OF WALK YOU WALK
WITH THE BABY CARRIAGE
MAKES YOU THE ENVY OF THE FOLKS YOU KNOW

GOOD FORTUNE'S FOUND YOU CHAPPIE
AND YOUR HEART'S A HAPPY VALENTINE
WHEN YOU'RE WALKING HAPPY
DON'T THE BLOOMIN' WORLD SEEM FINE!

   (Soft shoe dance as WILL begins to
   gather the items on the list)

WHEN YOU'RE WALKING HAPPY,
DON'T THE BLOOMIN' WORLD SEEM FINE!

   (Dance section)
THERE'S THE KIND OF WALK YOU WALK
WHEN YOU'VE GOT TO SCURRY
THERE'S THE KIND OF WALK YOU WALK, WALK YOU WALK, WALK YOU
   WALK
WHEN YOU'RE AFRAID THAT YOU ARE LATE

THERE'S THE KIND OF WALK YOU WALK
WHEN YOU'RE KIND OF LAZY
AND EVERY DAISY STOPS TO CONTEMPLATE
YOUR HAZY STATE

GOOD FORTUNE'S FOUND YOU CHAPPIE
AND YOUR HEART'S A HAPPY VALENTINE
WHEN YOU'RE WALKING HAPPY, WHEN YOU'RE WALKING HAPPY,
WHEN YOU'RE WALKING HAPPY

   (Tic-Toc)

ALL (Continued)

DON'T THE BLOOMIN' WORLD SEEM FINE WHEN YOU'RE WALKING HAPPY
DON'T THE BLOOMIN' WORLD SEEM FINE WHEN YOU'RE WALKING HAPPY
DON'T THE BLOOMIN' WORLD SEEM FINE WHEN YOU'RE WALKING HAPPY
DON'T THE BLOOMIN' WORLD SEEM FINE WHEN YOU'RE WALKING HAPPY
DON'T THE BLOOMIN' WORLD SEEM FINE WHEN YOU'RE WALKING HAPPY
DON'T THE BLOOMIN' WORLD SEEM FINE

LAST GROUP

WHEN YOU'RE WALKING HAPPY

      (As the LAST GROUP exits, WILL enters
      with a loaded cart which lifts him
      into the air)

WILL

DON'T THE BLOOMIN' WORLD SEEM FINE !!!

ACT II

Scene 4

>   WILL and MAGGIE's cellar. It is
>   evening and the place is clean.
>   MAGGIE is seated at an improvised
>   table, sewing a rip in WILL's
>   jacket. WILL enters from the
>   bedroom, exhausted.

                    WILL
The bed's up ... if you'll excuse me for mentioning it ...

                    MAGGIE
Thank you, Will.

                    WILL
This is not a very cheerful place for you to be living,
Miss Maggie.

                    MAGGIE
It's clean, and by the time we're together, it'll seem more
cheerful.

                    WILL
Well, I'll be getting along to Tubby's now.

                    MAGGIE
Sit down. You can work on your slate while I finish your
jacket.

                    WILL
My slate? Tonight? But I've had such a hard day.

                    MAGGIE
Good habits are made by finding no exceptions. I've written
a phrase for you to copy out.

>   (WILL sighs, picks up the slate, and
>   sits at other end of table)

"Love makes better that which is best."

                    WILL
"Love makes better that which is best."
>   (HE applies himself to writing with
>   great difficulty. After a moment,
>   HE looks up, shrugs. The lights
>   dim and HE sings introspectively:
>   "I DON'T THINK I'M IN LOVE")

"I DON'T THINK I'M IN LOVE"

WILL

(Sings)

VERSE:

SHE'S AT ME DAY AND NIGHT
SHE DON'T GIVE ME A CHANCE
LEARNED ME TO READ AND WRITE
NOW SHE'S LEARNING ME ROMANCE

I DON'T KNOW WHAT LOVE IS
WHICH IS HER MAIN COMPLAINT
I DON'T KNOW WHAT LOVE IS
BUT I SURE KNOW WHAT IT AIN'T, --

CHORUS:

I DON'T THINK I'M IN LOVE
I DON'T THINK I'M IN LOVE NOT NEARLY
FOLKS IN LOVE ACT KIND OF QUEERLY
I DON'T THINK I'M IN LOVE!

I DON'T THINK THERE'S A CHANCE
I DON'T THINK THAT WE'LL DANCE ON RAINBOWS
PEOPLE JUST DON'T DANCE ON RAINBOWS
I DON'T THINK I'M IN LOVE!

ALL I KNOW IS I DON'T FEEL FAINT OR WARMLY
ALL I KNOW IS I FEEL LIKE I FELT FORM'LY -- NORM'LY --

I DON'T THINK I'M IN LOVE
I WON'T SIGH IF I'M NOT AROUND HER
I'M A REAL UNGRATEFUL BOUNDER
STRING ME UP! HAVE ME SHOT!
DRAW AND QUARTER ME -- I'M NOT!!!

> (WILL sighs, then goes back to work-
> ing on his slate. MAGGIE looks
> across at WILL and sings intro-
> spectively)

MAGGIE

(Sings)
DOESN'T THINK HE'S IN LOVE
DOESN'T THINK HE'S IN LOVE NOT BARELY

> (WILL rubs out what HE wrote on
> slate and looks up)

WILL

IF I SIGH IT'S VERY RARELY
(Starts to write again)

                    MAGGIE
DOESN'T THINK HE'S IN LOVE

DOESN'T THINK HE'S ON CLOUDS
DOESN'T THINK HE SEES CROWDS OF BLUE BIRDS

          (WILL again rubs out slate and
          looks up)

                    WILL
FRANKLY I SEE VERY FEW BIRDS

                    MAGGIE
DOESN'T THINK HE'S IN LOVE

          (WILL begins to fall asleep)

FROM THE START I TOLD HIM WHERE HE WAS HEADED
KNOW THAT HE'LL BE MINE, ONCE I GET HIM WEDDED -- BEDDED --

DOESN'T THINK HE'S IN LOVE
DOESN'T THINK THAT THE FEELING'S FOUND HIM
AH! BUT WITH MY ARMS AROUND HIM
HE'LL WAKE UP TO WHAT'S WHAT
WHO IS HE TO THINK HE'S NOT!!!

          (After the song MAGGIE bites off
          the thread)

                    MAGGIE
Willie?
          (SHE rises and goes to WILL with
          the jacket)
Willie. You'd best be getting on to Tubby's now.

                    WILL
Don't you want to correct my slate?

                    MAGGIE
          (Looks at the slate)
You're coming along, my lad.

          (The door opens. An OLD WOMAN
          enters. WILL and MAGGIE are
          mesmerized)

                    WOMAN
I saw your sign. Are you still open?

                    MAGGIE
Oh yes, madam ... Indeed we are.

                    WOMAN
I've just had a little accident. A broken lace. Could
you ...   — 73 —

                    WILL
          (Grabbing a chair)
Aye, mum. Will you have a seat, mum. Laces, Miss Maggie ..

          (MAGGIE goes to the makeshift
          counter. The WOMAN sits down)

Pleasant evening, isn't it, mum? A little on the cool side,
but if it weren't on the cool side this time of year, it'd
undoubtedly be on the warm side ... and, if there be a
choice, I think it be better on the cool side ... at least
for this time of year ...

          (MAGGIE has come back to the WOMAN
          and waits for WILL to finish)

                    MAGGIE
I think these 'ull do ...

                    WOMAN
Yes. They're very nice. How much ... ?

                    MAGGIE
Just a penny ...

          (The WOMAN hands MAGGIE a penny)

Thank you, Madam. And come again.

                    WOMAN
          (Rising)
I will. You two seem so eager to please ...

                    WILL
We are that, mum. Mind the step, mum.

                    WOMAN
Good night.

                    WILL
Good night, mum ... madam.

          (The WOMAN goes. MAGGIE hands WILL
          the penny and gets cash box.

                                        Piano Score No. 15A
          Looking at the penny)   Page 182
Our first penny ... By Gum!

                    MAGGIE
Into the box, Will ...

                    WILL
You should be the one to put it in, Miss Maggie.

                    — 74 —

                              MAGGIE
No. You do it.

                    (WILL puts the penny gravely into
                    the cash box)

It's a beginning.

                              WILL
Aye. It's a beginning, Miss Maggie.
                    (HE puts box down)

                              MAGGIE
There's another thing we should be beginning, Will. It's
Maggie from now on.

                              WILL
It is?

                              MAGGIE
Aye. Now, off with you ...

                    (WILL reaches out for scarf. SHE
                    puts it around his neck rather
                    affectionately)

                              WILL
Thank you, Miss Maggie ...

                              MAGGIE
Maggie ...

                              WILL
Maggie ...
                    (HE goes.

                    MAGGIE looks after him a moment.
                    WILL pauses outside and looks up
                    at the sign)

                              MAGGIE
                    (Sings)
HE DOES NOT BELIEVE THAT HIS HEART CAN FLUTTER
BUT BEFORE TOO LONG WORDS OF LOVE HE'LL MUTTER ...
    STUTTER ...

                              WILL
I DON'T THINK I'M IN LOVE
SHOULD I SAY IT SHE'D JUST OUT-SHOUT ME

                              MAGGIE
AH BUT CAN HE DO WITHOUT ME

                              — 75 —

                              WILL
HOW'D I GET WHERE I GOT

                         MAGGIE
WHO IS HE TO THINK HE'S NOT

              (WILL goes off)

                    FADE OUT

ACT II

Scene 5

Three weeks later. Afternoon.
Exterior Moonrakers -- DENTON,
TUDSBURY and HEELER are at Stage R.
BOY with handbills crosses to them.
Hands them a handbill.

DENTON

What's this about?

BOY

For the new Bootmaker.

DENTON

(Reading)
"Attention all footsufferers. If through previous poor fit
or stiff leather you have been exposed to the pain and
anguish of aching feet, your troubles have come to an end.
I am pleased to offer fine boots, guaranteed to comfort and
durability. Why pay more and suffer? All work done under
my personal direction. William Mossop, Master Bootmaker."

HEELER

Has Henry seen this?

DENTON

I don't think so. He's in pub already.

HEELER

I would be too if my girl ran off with a boothand.

(THEY are crossing to HOBSON in the
Moonrakers. The place is filled
with MEN taking their beer break.
HOBSON, who is slightly drunk, is
seated, a bottle of whiskey in
front of him)

Well, Henry, I hear things have been a bit slow for you
these past few weeks.

HOBSON

Don't worry about me, Heeler.

DENTON

But you've got some real competition in Salford now ...

                    HOBSON
A cat can look at a king, Denton, but he still crawls for
scraps.
          (To TUDSBURY)
And, as for those who have shown disloyalty by doing such
things as letting space to the competition ... it'll be a
long time before they see my brass again.

                    TUDSBURY
Maggie's brass is as good as yours, Henry. And it comes in
regular.

                    HOBSON
They won't last. Carriage trade always came to Hobson's
and always will.

                    DENTON
I hear Mrs. Hepworth has been in to Maggie's twice in the
past three weeks ...

                    HOBSON
One swallow doesn't make a summer. Come on, Heeler, have a
drink with me.

                    HEELER
I don't drink whiskey this time of day, Henry.

                    TUDSBURY
It's not my business, Henry, but a tradesman can't afford to
have hard liquor on his breath during shop ...

                    HOBSON
You're right, Tudsbury ... it's not your business ...

          (BOY enters the saloon with a pack
          of handbills and comes to the table
          to hand them out)

What's that?

                    BOY
From the new bootmaker.

                    HOBSON
I can read.

                    DENTON
Attention all footsufferers ...

                    HOBSON
I said I can read ... Here, lad ... just a minute ... I'll
take those.
          (Grabbing handbills from the BOY)

                      - 78 -

                                    BOY
But sir, they paid me a shilling to hand them out ...

                                  HOBSON
Here's two shillings not to hand them out. That's the way
Hobson takes care of competition.

                    (The BOY takes the money and starts
                    off. HE stops at the door and takes
                    another sheaf of handbills from under
                    his jacket)

Whatchya doing ... ?

                                    BOY
They paid me another shilling to hand these out after you
paid me two shillings not to hand those out.

                    (HOBSON reacts with a groan. The
                    BOY goes)

                                  HEELER
She knows you like her own hand, Henry, and that's a fact.
Well, come on. We've shops to attend.

                    (The MEN rise and start to go)

Coming, Henry ... ?

                                  HOBSON
Nay, I'm not. With Maggie off me, I come and go as I please.

                    (The MEN go)

I'm free, that's what I am ... free.

                    (BEENSTOCK enters and crosses to
                    HOBSON's table)

                                BEENSTOCK
Hobson, you're going to hell, you know that ...
                    (HE starts to sit)

                                  HOBSON
Did I invite you to my table ... ?

                                BEENSTOCK
Remember the day when you told me I was leading you away
from all this ...

                                  HOBSON
Shall I ever forget it? It was the start of lawyers and
settlements and revolution in the ranks. Now, get away
from me, Beenstock, before I lose my temper ...

                    BEENSTOCK
Hobson, this devilish brew is leading you to eternal
damnation. Unless you change your ways, the demons of hell
will pursue you forever ...

                    HOBSON
I prefer their company to yours ... Now, leave me alone ...

                    BEENSTOCK
Hobson, I beg of you ...

                    HOBSON
Get away from me, you buttoned-up glass of water you.
          (HE starts to rise and attack
          BEENSTOCK)
Go on -- get out of here!

          (BEENSTOCK goes.

          HOBSON tries to pour another drink
          but finds the bottle empty)
Minns ... another bottle.

          (MINNS leaves another bottle on the
          table and HOBSON sits and falls into
          sleep. LIGHTS change to indicate a
          passage of time.

          HOBSON then wakes with a start and
          reaches for his watch)
What's the time?
          (HE tries to pour from the second
          bottle and finds that it, too, is
          empty. HE rises and goes to the
          bar)   Piano Score No. 16
Minns ... another bottle.   Page 187

          (TWO MINNS now appear behind the
          bar, EACH holding a bottle)

                    MINNS AND DOUBLE
I'm not sure I should let you have this, Henry ...

                    HOBSON
          (Recoiling)
Minns, you run a pleasant establishment here. But start
playing tricks on your regular customers and you can turn
this place into livery stable.

                    MINNS AND DOUBLE
No need to get nasty, Henry.

          (TWO SNAKES come up over the edge
          of the bar)

                    — 80 —

                          HOBSON
Ooo ... look. It's about time you did something about the
vermin in here ...
                (HE hits at them with his pocket
                handkerchief)
Shoo ... get out ... They're coming in from the river.

            (FOUR IMAGINARY DEVILS now appear
            and greet HOBSON)

        "SUCH A SOCIABLE SORT"

                      (THE DEVILS)
            (Sing)
VERSE:
                        1st DEVIL
HOW DO YOU DO?

                        2nd DEVIL
HOW DO YOU DO?

                        3rd DEVIL
HOW DO YOU DO?

                        4th DEVIL
HOW DO YOU DO?

                      ALL
IT CAN'T BE ESTIMATED
THE YEARS THAT WE HAVE WAITED, FOR YOU, -- JUST FOR YOU!

AND YOU CAN'T GUESS HOW DELIGHTED
WE ARE TO BE INVITED, DEAR FRIEND, -- TO ATTEND

IT WAS WORTH EV'RY BIT OF THE CLIMB
WE SHOULD HAVE US A 'DEVILISH' TIME, --

CHORUS:

IT'S A RARE AND A TOTAL TREAT
WHAT A MARVELOUS MAN TO MEET
            (Pause)
SUCH A SOCIABLE SORT

WITH A QUALITY THAT DEMANDS
SLAPPING SHOULDERS AND SHAKING HANDS
            (Pause)
SUCH A SOCIABLE SORT
            (Pause)
KINDLY BRING HIM A QUART

THE ART OF CAROUSING -- NOTHING TRIVIAL
YOU'RE CONGEN'YAL AND -- SO CONVIVIAL

                    — 81 —

A ROLLICKER NONE CAN BEAT
YOU ARE SWEEPING US OFF OUR FEET
WE SHOULD HAVE US A TIME BEFORE WE'RE THROUGH

GIVE A CHEER

                        HOBSON
HEAR! HEAR!

                        THE DEVILS
NO ONE COMES NEAR
SUCH A SOCIABLE SORT
SUCH A PERFECTLY ELEGANT SPORT
SUCH A SOCIABLE SORT, -- LIKE YOU!!!

        (HOBSON and DEVILS dance)

CHORUS: (2)

YOU'RE ALWAYS SO VERY -- BACCHANALIAN
YOU MAKE NERO SEEM -- 'PISCOPALIAN

A MAN WE CAN COMPREHEND
AND A ROISTERER TO THE END
ONE WOULD THINK THAT ANY DRINK YOU DRINK IS FREE

GIVE A CHEER!

                        HOBSON
HEAR! HEAR!

                        THE DEVILS
YOU HAVE NO PEER
SUCH A SOCIABLE SORT

                        HOBSON
LIKE ME!!!

        (DEVILS dance out of Moonrakers
        leading HOBSON to street)

ACT II

Scene 6

Exterior of BEENSTOCK's Corn Ware-
house. An open delivery chute is
downstage. The choreography ends
as the DEVILS cause HOBSON to lose
his balance and slide down the
chute.

THE DEVILS

CHORUS: (3)

IF WE HAD TO SUM UP -- YOU'RE ADORABLE
YOU'RE SO SODOM-LIKE -- AND GOMMORABLE

DISRAELI IS THRU AND DONE
HE WAS NEVER YOUR MATCH FOR FUN
AS A ROUNDER HE CANNOT QUALIFY

GIVE A CHEER!

HOBSON

HEAR! HEAR!

THE DEVILS

IT'S ALL TOO CLEAR
SUCH A SOCIABLE SORT
AND A MAN THAT WE'LL HAVE TO SUPPORT
SUCH A SOCIABLE SORT, --

HOBSON

LIKE I!

(After the number, DEVILS lead HOBSON
to a chain guarding BEENSTOCK's grain
elevator, remove the chain and cause
him to slide down)

DEVILS

SUCH A SOCIABLE SORT
LIKE YOU!

ACT II

Scene 7

ALICE and VICKIE are in postures
of abject depression. TUBBY is
straightening the shop.

TUBBY

Well, what's it to be, Miss Vickie? Clogs? Ladies' boots?
Men's boots for stock? What am I to make today?

VICKIE

Oh, what difference does it make?

TUBBY

If you want to stay in business, you have to give orders.

VICKIE

I don't care whether we stay in business or not. You're the
foreman. You decide what to make.

TUBBY

A foreman fores. He doesn't give orders. You give orders.
I fore. That's the way it works. I'd give a week's wages
to have Miss Maggie back running shop again.

VICKIE

I'm sick of hearing about the shop. It's the two of us that
really need Maggie's help.

TUBBY
(Sympathetically)
I know. Is there anything I can do?

ALICE

Tubby, you're a fine boothand, but I don't think you'd be
much use in affairs of the heart.

TUBBY

Aye, you're right.
(Looking around. Lifts trap)
Well, I never thought I'd see the day when everything around
here would go to the rack and ruin it's going to.
(TUBBY goes down the trap.

MAGGIE and WILL enter)

MAGGIE

Oh, I'm glad to see Hobson's is so busy this morning.

VICKIE

Maggie, we're so glad to see you.

ALICE
(Placing a chair for her)
Here. Sit down.

VICKIE
(Ushering her to it)
Yes, do sit down.

MAGGIE

Oh, well, thank you.
(SHE sits)
Where's father?

ALICE

Oh, he never comes down till noon these days.

VICKIE

Oh, Maggie, I certainly hope you've thought of something to set things right for us.

MAGGIE

Nay, as a matter of fact, I haven't. I've been too busy setting things right for myself. But when that's done, I'll put my mind to your problems. Meanwhile, I've come to invite you to my wedding. Two o'clock today. At church.

VICKIE
(Horrified)
No!

ALICE

Not today!

MAGGIE
(Hardening at their reaction)
Today! Now, Alice, you can sell me something. There are some brass rings in that drawer there.

ALICE

You're not marrying with a brass ring?!
(ALICE goes to the drawer and takes
out a case of rings. MAGGIE picks
one out)

MAGGIE

I am. Will and me is not throwing our money around.
(SHE tries several on)
This one will do nicely.
(SHE puts down some coins)
Here's thruppence ...

                    ALICE
The rings are fourpence, Maggie ...

                    MAGGIE
But you'll take thruppence. I'm entitlted to wholesale ...

                    VICKIE
I never thought you'd go through with it, Maggie ...

                    ALICE
It makes things even worse for us, you know ...

                    MAGGIE
No, I don't see that ...

                    VICKIE
Well, look again. Suppose, somehow, we can change father's
mind.

                    MAGGIE
What's that got to do with Will and me?

                    VICKIE
We'll then have a brother-in-law who's sure to give the
Beenstocks second thoughts about the Hobsons ...

                    WILL
I'm sorry, Miss Vickie ... Excuse me, Miss Alice. I really
had no intention to ...

                    MAGGIE
Stop apologizing, Will. And they're Alice and Vickie now.

                    ALICE
Now, Maggie, that's a bit much ...

                    MAGGIE
Maybe so, but do you two want my help in future?

                    ALICE
Of course, Maggie ...

                    VICKIE
Well, yes.

                    MAGGIE
Then you'll start being respectful to my Will and right now.

                    ALICE
It's not easy, Maggie. After all, Will Mossop was our
boothand.

                    MAGGIE
Aye, he was. But he's as good as you now. And better.

WILL

Nay, come now, Miss Maggie ...

MAGGIE

Ay, better, I say. They're shop assistants. You're your
own master.

WILL

I got my name written on front of shop alright, but I don't
know so much about being my own master.

MAGGIE

If that's what it says, that's what you are.
      (TO SISTERS)
Now -- you can both kiss him for your brother-in-law to be!

WILL

Nay, Miss Maggie. I'm no great hand at kissing.

MAGGIE

I've noticed that. A bit of practice will do you no harm.
Come along, Alice.

ALICE

I won't do it.

MAGGIE

I'm waiting.

WILL

I don't see that you ought to drive her to it.

MAGGIE

You hold your hush. She's making up her mind to it.

WILL

I'd just as soon not put her to the trouble.

MAGGIE

You'll take your proper place in this family, my lad,
trouble or no trouble. Come along, Alice, I've got a lot
of things to do today, and you're holding everything back.

ALICE

It's under protest.

MAGGIE

Protest, but kiss.

      (ALICE reluctantly kisses WILL)

Your turn, Vickie.

                              VICKIE
I don't see why you should always get your way.

                              MAGGIE
It's a habit. Will's waiting. Kiss him hearty.

               (VICKIE kisses WILL quickly)

                              WILL
By Gum, there's more to kissing young women than I thought.

                              MAGGIE
Don't get too fond of it, my lad.

          (The street door opens and FREDDIE
               enters in great excitement)

                              VICKIE
Freddie, what are you doing here?

                              ALICE
What if father comes down ... ?

                              FREDDIE
He won't. You know where your father is?

                              VICKIE
Why, upstairs, of course ...

                              FREDDIE
No, he's not. He's in our corn cellar ... asleep. He must
have slid down chute last night after coming out of Moonrakers.

                              ALICE
Is he hurt?

                              FREDDIE
He's snoring very loud, but he isn't hurt. He fell on some
soft bags ...

                              VICKIE
It's shameful. We'd best go and get him.

                              MAGGIE
No. Wait a minute.
          (To FREDDIE)
You say he fell in your corn cellar. After coming out of
the Moonrakers? And he's still asleep?

                              FREDDIE
That's right.

                    MAGGIE
Did he cause any damage?

                    FREDDIE
Well, he did break open some corn bags, but I don't ...

                    MAGGIE
I wonder ... knowing Father ... maybe this is the
opportunity ...

                    VICKIE
What are you talking about, Maggie?

                    MAGGIE
Get me pencil and paper ...

               (ALICE scurries to the desk and
               hands MAGGIE paper and pencil.

          MAGGIE begins to write)
It all seems to add up. Father'll say it's a plot against
the middle class, but it might just be a way to make things
work out for the four of you.

                    ALICE
Maggie, tell us ...

                    MAGGIE
There isn't time. You'll find out soon enough.
          (SHE hands the paper to FREDDIE)
Here, take this to Albert and tell him to follow these
directions exactly. After that you're both to meet Will
and me at church at two o'clock. You and Albert will stand
on the groom's side.

                    FREDDIE
You're getting married today, Maggie?

          (MAGGIE nods)

Best wishes, Maggie.
          (HE turns and goes to WILL)
Congratulations, Will.
          (FREDDIE picks up WILL's limp hand,
          shakes it and goes. WILL smiles
          wanly)

                    MAGGIE
He could turn out to be a nice young man.

                    ALICE
Maggie, you've got to tell us what you wrote on that paper.

                    — 89 —

MAGGIE

I said there isn't time.
(Crosses to trap and stamps on it)
Go upstairs and get dressed. I'll be along in a minute.

(VICKIE and ALICE go into the house)

Here's the ring, Will. Now, you're to hold it until it's time to slip it on my finger.

WILL
(Taking the ring gingerly)
Aye ... I'm aware of the custom.

MAGGIE

You're looking a bit green, my lad.

WILL

I am?

MAGGIE

Is it second thoughts you're having?

WILL

Second thoughts? Nay, Miss Maggie ... Maggie. I'm going through with it. I've wrought myself up to the point, and by gum, I'm ready.

MAGGIE

You're going into a church, you know, not to the dentist.

WILL

That's true enough. You get rid of sumnat at dentist.

TUBBY
(Coming up from the trap)
Why, it's Miss Maggie.

MAGGIE

Come on up, Tubby. You're in charge of shop. The girls will be gone for a time.

TUBBY

Very well, Miss Maggie.

(MAGGIE exits into the house)

Hello, Will.

WILL

Don't you "hello, Will" me.

TUBBY

What's the matter with you?

WILL

Tubby, I just want you to know that I'm holding you
responsible for what's happened to me.

TUBBY

You're going through with it, then.

WILL

She's going through with it. I'm being dragged.

TUBBY

Well, she's not the worst you could get.

(SONG: "IT MIGHT AS WELL BE HER")

"IT MIGHT AS WELL BE HER"   Piano Score No. 17
                                   Page 206

TUBBY

(Sings)

LOVE AT BEST IS ALWAYS FILLED WITH DOUBT
LOVE'S A GAMBLE AS IT WERE-ER
SINCE THERE'S NO WAY YOU CAN WRIGGLE OUT
IT MIGHT AS WELL BE HER!

LOVE CAN BRING A LEMON OR A PLUM
LOVE DON'T ASK WHICH YOU PREFER-ER
EITHER ONE CAN TALK YOU DEAF AND DUMB

TUBBY & WILL

IT MIGHT AS WELL BE HER!

WILL

I'M AWARE THAT THE HONOR'S RARE
I COULD SHIRK BUT I WON'T
AS I STAND WITH THE RING IN HAND
I'LL TELL HIM I DO, ALTHOUGH I DON'T

IF I HAVE TO HONOR AND OBEY
THANKS TO YOU, DEAR SIR
I DON'T DENY MY FRIGHT
BUT I'M TOO WEAK TO FIGHT
SO WRONG OR RIGHT IT MIGHT AS WELL BE HER

TUBBY

IT'S QUITE NICE, WHEN THEY THROW THE RICE

WILL

AND YOU START LIFE'S DUET
FOR HER SAKE, YOU EAT WEDDING CAKE

TUBBY

THE LAST TASTE OF SWEETNESS YOU WILL GET

— 91 —

                              WILL
IF I LEFT HER WAITING AT THE CHURCH

                              TUBBY
YOU'D BE QUITE THE CUR

                              WILL & TUBBY
SO RING THE WEDDING BELL
AND LET THE CHOIR YELL   Piano Score No. 17A
OH, WHAT THE HELL   Page 215
IT MIGHT AS WELL BE HER!

                    FADE OUT

Piano Score No. 17B
                                 Page 217

                    The elevator rises out of the pit.
                    On it, amid broken sacks of feed
                    and grain, is HOBSON. HE is sleep-
                    ing. FREDDIE and ALBERT enter.
                    ALBERT hands writ to FREDDIE.
                    FREDDIE crosses to HOBSON and
                    starts to pin on writ.

                         HOBSON
                    (Starts to wake up)
Here, here.
                    (HE settles back to sleep and FREDDIE
                    finishes pinning on writ. FREDDIE
                    taps HOBSON to wake him up)

                         FREDDIE
Good morning, Mr. Hobson.
                    (HE leaves)

                         HOBSON
Morning. Who's that?
                    (HE becomes aware of the blue paper
                    and tears it off)
What is this ... ? Action ... action for damages? What
action ...
                    (HE opens it and reads it)
Henry Horatio Hobson is charged with trespassing on the
premises of Beenstock's Corn Merchant of Chapel Street ...
                    (HE stops, reads further)
The plaintive Beenstock demands damages ...
                    (HE stops)
Why, those dirty scheming two-faced lawyers ...
                    (HE sinks back on the sacks)
If they think they can squeeze me ...
                    (HE pauses, considering)
Oh, maybe they can ... maybe they can ...

ACT II

Scene 9

The Mossop Bootery, now completely
furnished. On the table is a
wedding cake. WILL is at one end
of the table, MAGGIE at the other.
ALICE, VICKIE, FREDDIE and ALBERT
are ranged along its sides.

                    FREDDIE
To the Bride.

                    ALBERT
To the Bridegroom.

                    ALL FOUR
Long life and Happiness.

                    VICKIE
Bless you, Maggie.

                    ALICE
And you to, Will.

                    MAGGIE
Willie ...

                    WILL
Ah, well ... it's a very great pleasure to see you here
today. It's an honor you do us, and I assure you, speaking
for my ... my wife, as well as for myself, that the ...
uh ... the ...

                    MAGGIE
Generous ...

                    WILL
Oh, aye, that's right. That the generous warmth of the
sentiments so cordially expressed by Mr. Albert Beenstock
... and so enthusiastically seconded by ... no, I've gotten
that wrong road round.

        (Laughter)

Expressed by Mr. Freddie Beenstock ... and seconded by Mr.
Albert Beenstock ... will never be forgotten by either my
... life partner ... or self. And I'd like to drink this
toast to you in my own house. Our guests, and may they all
soon be married soon themselves. And that's the end.

                    (Applause. WILL and MAGGIE toast
                    the OTHERS with their teacups.

                    HOBSON knocks on the street door)

                              MAGGIE
Oh, he's right on time.

                    (HOBSON knocks again)

                              HOBSON
                    (Off)
Maggie ... are you there?

                              ALICE
                    (Terrified)
It's Father ...

                              VICKIE
What'll we do ... ?

                              MAGGIE
Into the bedroom, all of you. I'll call when I want you.
Take your cups.

                    (THEY all start for the bedroom,
                    including WILL)

Not you, Will. Sit.

                    (THEY all go. WILL sits and MAGGIE
                    goes to the street door and opens it.
                    HOBSON is revealed on the top step)

                              HOBSON
                    (With slight apology)
Well, Maggie ...

                              MAGGIE
                    (Uninvitingly)
Well, Father.

                              HOBSON
I'll come in.

                              MAGGIE
                    (Standing in his way)
Well, I don't know about that. I'll have to ask the master.

                              HOBSON
The master?

                              MAGGIE
                    (To WILL)
Will, it's my father. Is he to come in?

                            WILL
          (Loud and bold)
Aye, let him come in.

                    (HOBSON comes in, crosses and sits
                    in the chair next to WILL. As HE
                    raises his hand to take off his
                    hat, WILL flinches)

                            HOBSON
          (Perplexed)
What's the matter with you?

                            WILL
          (Recovering)
I'm just pleased to see you, Mr. Hobson ...
          (Grabs HOBSON's hand and pumps it)
It makes our wedding day complete like, you being her
father ...

                            HOBSON
          (Cuts in)
Wedding day ... ?

                            MAGGIE
Aye. You're a bit late for the wedding do, but we are glad
to see you just the same ...

                            HOBSON
Maggie, I've no time for the unimportant. I'm in trouble
... serious trouble.

                            MAGGIE
          (Cutting the cake)
I'm sure it's serious ...

                            HOBSON
Well, then, pay attention ...

                            MAGGIE
But I've a wish to see my father sitting at my table ...

                            HOBSON
Because there isn't much time ...

                            MAGGIE
Sitting at my table, eating my wedding cake ...

                            HOBSON
Maggie, listen to me ...

                            MAGGIE
Eating my wedding cake on my wedding day.

                    HOBSON
Maggie, listen to me. There'll be lawyers swarming around
again ... take the very meat off my bones ...

                    MAGGIE
          (Carefully measured)
Sit down ... Father.

          (HOBSON looks MAGGIE in the eye)

                    HOBSON
Aye ... I see what you mean ...
          (HE sits.

          MAGGIE places a piece of cake on a
          plate and pushes it toward HOBSON)

                    MAGGIE
Here's your piece of cake and you can eat it.

                    HOBSON
          (Pushes it back)
Maggie, I give you my word, there's no ill feeling.

                    MAGGIE
          (Pushes it back to him)
Then we'll have the deed.

                    HOBSON
Not just now, Maggie.

                    MAGGIE
You will eat the cake and wish us well, Father.

                    HOBSON
You're a hard woman.
          (HE takes a bit of the cake and
          chews it with a grimace and swallows
          with difficulty)

                    MAGGIE
And wish us well ...

                    HOBSON
All right, I'll say this: when a thing's done, it's done.
I'm none proud of the choice you made. But compared to the
troubles I've got, it don't bother me as much as it should.

                    WILL
We thank you for your blessings, Mr. Hobson.

                    HOBSON
Pass the tea, will you.
          (HE drinks)

MAGGIE

Now, then, father, was there something you wanted to talk
about?

(HOBSON hands MAGGIE the subpoena)

HOBSON

Maggie, I'm in trouble, bad trouble. It's those lawyers
again with their evil minds and scheming ways.

MAGGIE

Better to show it to my husband, I think.
          (Takes the paper and hands it to
          WILL)

HOBSON

But, Maggie, that's private ...

MAGGIE

Private from Will? Nay, it isn't. Me and Will is as one
now. And the sooner you understand that the better.

HOBSON

Will Mossop ...

WILL

Sit down, Mr. Hobson.

(HOBSON sits)

MAGGIE

From now on you call him father ...

WILL

Do I ... ?

HOBSON

Does he ... ?

MAGGIE

He does ...

WILL

Miss Maggie, I think you'd better have a look at this, too.
          (HE hands MAGGIE the paper)

MAGGIE

Aye ... It's an action for damages and trespass, I see ...

HOBSON

It's an unfair, un-English way of taking advantage of a
casual accident ...

MAGGIE

Did you destroy property in Beenstock's cellar? Did you trespass?

HOBSON
(Whining)

I had an accident, Maggie, I don't deny it. I stayed too long at Moonrakers ...

MAGGIE

Oh. It is serious. I shouldn't wonder you'll lose some trade from this.

HOBSON

Wonder! It's as certain as Christmas if I have to stand up in open court and admit I was overcome in public street.

WILL

Do you think it will get into paper?

MAGGIE

Maybe the Salford Reporter?

HOBSON

The Salford Reporter?! A man of my standing ... The Manchester Guardian ... !

WILL

By gum, think of that! It's very near worthwhile to be ruined for the pleasure of reading about yourself in Manchester Guardian.

HOBSON

It's there for others to read about besides me ...

WILL

Aye, you're right. I didn't think of that. This 'ull give alot of satisfaction to a many I could name. Other people's troubles is mostly what folks read the paper for, and I reckon it's twice the pleasure to them when it's the troubles of a man they know personally.

HOBSON

To hear you talk, it sounds like a pleasure to you ...

WILL

Nay, it's not. But I always think it's best to look on the worst side of things first, then whatever happens can't be worse than you first looked for.

HOBSON

I'm getting a lot of comfort from your husband, Maggie ...

                              WILL
I only spoke what came into my mind.

                              HOBSON
Have you got any more consolation for me?

                              WILL
Well, I'll admit I'm not much good at talking and I always
seem to say the wrong thing when I do talk.

                              HOBSON
You certainly do.

                              WILL
Well, I'm sorry if my well-meant words don't suit your
taste, but I thought you came here for my advice.

                              HOBSON
             (Explodes)
I didn't come here to talk to you, you grimy cock-a-
hoop ... !

                              MAGGIE
Sit down, father. My husband is just trying to help you.

                              HOBSON
Tell him not to strain himself.

                              MAGGIE
Now, then, this trespass is going to cost you something,
you know ...

                              HOBSON
But, Maggie, being dragged into a court of law ... and the
newspapers ...
             (HE shudders)

                              MAGGIE
Cases have been settled out of court ...

                              HOBSON
I've been through that. Set foot in lawyer's office and
they squeeze you twice as hard in private as they dare do
in public.

                              MAGGIE
You might not have to go to court ... or to a lawyer's
office, father.

                              HOBSON
What do you mean, Maggie?

             (BEENSTOCK knocks)

                              MAGGIE
It can be settled right here.
                    (SHE rises and goes to the door)

                              HOBSON
                    (Suspicious)
Right here ... ?

                    (MAGGIE opens the door. BEENSTOCK
                    enters. A groan from HOBSON)

Oh, no ...

                              BEENSTOCK
Good evening, Hobson ...

                    (MAGGIE goes to bedroom door and
                    opens it. The FOUR YOUNG PEOPLE
                    come out. HOBSON is startled)

                              HOBSON
Alice ... Vickie ... what's all this? What are you lot
doing here?

                              BEENSTOCK
I think you know Freddie, my son and business associate ...

                              FREDDIE
Mr. Hobson ...

                    (HOBSON groans again)

                              BEENSTOCK
And my son, Albert ... my solicitor.

                              ALBERT
Mr. Hobson ...

                              HOBSON
A solicitor ... at his age ...

                              BEENSTOCK
Well, Hobson, shall we get down to business?

                              HOBSON
Don't abuse a noble word, Beenstock. Honest men live by
business. Thieves like you live by law ...

                              ALBERT
I wish to remind you, Mr. Hobson, that abuse of the
plaintiff is remembered in the costs ...

                    (HOBSON grunst in frustration.
                    BEENSTOCK places his hand on
                    FREDDIE's shoulder)
                          — 101 —

BEENSTOCK

Now, I want to assure you, Hobson, that neither I nor the
assistant manager of Beenstock's, has any wish to be
vindictive. Though you committed a trespass, caused damage
to stock and spied on trade secrets, we are all conscious
of your position in this community ... your reputation for
respectability ...

HOBSON

How much ... ?

BEENSTOCK

I beg your pardon ...

HOBSON

I'm not so fond of the sound of your voice as you are.
What's the sum?

BEENSTOCK

The sum we propose is one thousand pounds ...

HOBSON

What!

WILL

By gum!

MAGGIE

That's too much ... !

BEENSTOCK

We don't think so ...

MAGGIE

Well, think again. It's greedy. And if you insist on that
sum there'll be a counteraction for personal damages due to
your criminal carelessness in leaving your cellar flap open.

HOBSON

That's right, Maggie! You've saved me! I'll pay nothing!

MAGGIE

Yes, you will, father. You'll pay what you can afford.
And that's five hundred pounds.
        (To BEENSTOCK)
Is that acceptable?

BEENSTOCK

All right, five hundred pounds ... and ...
        (HE takes a blue rosette from his
        pocket)
... you agree to wear the blue rosette ...

                    HOBSON
Oh, no ... I don't ...

          (A tense pause. ALL eyes on HOBSON)

                    MAGGIE
Father, I've already saved you five hundred pounds. And
you won't have to go to court. Well, Father?

                    HOBSON
          (After a moment, and finally
          defeated)
What choice does an honest man have?

                    BEENSTOCK
Very well, then. I suggest that the money be paid in two
drafts of two hundred and fifty pounds each.

                    HOBSON
Two drafts ... ?

                    BEENSTOCK
          (Smiling)
Payable to Albert and Freddie ... as the settlements for
your two lovely daughters ...

          (Silence as THEY all watch HOBSON)

                    HOBSON
The settlements! I have been diddled!

                    MAGGIE
Well, what's it to be, Father? Court or courting?

                    HOBSON
All right. All right. You've got your settlements.

          (There is general elation among the
          FOUR YOUNG PEOPLE. THEY hug and
          kiss each other and MAGGIE. THEY
          kiss HOBSON who grumpily waves them
          away. BEENSTOCK follows them to
          the door and pauses)

                    BEENSTOCK
By the way.
          (HE crosses to HOBSON and places the
          blue rosette in HOBSON's lapel)
Henry Horatio Hobson's word is his bond ... remember?

          (HOBSON groans)

You've taken the first step to a new life, Henry ...

                    — 103 —

                              HOBSON
Aye, and the vision of it horrifies me ...

                    (BEENSTOCK goes.

                    HOBSON turns on MAGGIE, waving
                         a finger)
Well, Maggie, I know who I've got to thank for all this.

                              MAGGIE
You said they could wed Freddie and Albert, Father. And
as far as the blue rosette, it's for your own good, and
for the good of your business ...

                              HOBSON
My business is none of your business any more.
                    (Turns to WILL angrily)
And as for you, if you'll excuse my coarseness on your
wedding night, you've made your bed and now you can lie
in it!
                    (HOBSON starts for the door. WILL
                    winces slightly at the reference to
                    'bed,' looks at MAGGIE)

                              WILL
                    (To HOBSON at door)
Father ...

                    (HOBSON stops as if stabbed in the
                    back)

It's still early ...

                    (HOBSON turns. MAGGIE is puzzled)

I mean it's not time to ... How about another cup of tea?

                              HOBSON
                    (Wondering what's up)
You want me to stay?

                              WILL
                    (Stalling for time)
Aye. After all ... we men of the family ought to become
better acquainted ... since we be relatives and all ...
so to speak ... and there be things to talk about ...

                              HOBSON
                    (Regarding WILL suspiciously)
Relatives, eh ... ? Things to talk about? Are you two
coming to your senses at last? ... Well, better sooner than
later.
                    (HE looks around the shop)

                            — 104 —

HOBSON (Continued)

You thought it would be easy, didn't you. Hang out a sign
and fight off the carriage trade ... Instead you've ended
up in squalor, ten feet below ground, without a shilling,
crying for help ...

MAGGIE

Just a minute, father ...

HOBSON
(Going right on)

Well, no matter how ill you've used me, my soft heart always
takes command. We'll forget what's happened. You both can
come back to Hobson's. Willie, you'll go back to your old
bench. No cut in wages. Maggie, you'll keep house and run
shop. We'll go halves in the cost of food. Nothing extra
for what he eats as long as he keeps it within reason.
Could I make a more open-handed offer? Well, we can take
it as settled, right?

(MAGGIE starts to answer indignantly,
but before SHE can say anything, WILL
sings: "YOU'RE RIGHT")

"YOU'RE RIGHT, YOU'RE RIGHT"   Piano Score No. 18
                                      Page 221

(Reprise)

WILL
(Sings)

YOU'RE RIGHT! YOU'RE RIGHT! YOU'RE ABSOLUTELY RIGHT
VIEWING IT FROM YOUR POINT OF VIEW
I'M SURE YOU FEEL, YOU'VE OFFERED QUITE A DEAL
I SHOULD GO ALONG WITH YOU

HOW NICE TO GO BACK TO THE CELLAR
BACK UNDER THE FLOOR COLD AND DAMP
TO SIT THERE WITH TUBBY
ALL GRIMEY AND GRUBBY
JUST WAITING FOR YOU, SIR, TO STAMP

A POOR LITTLE IGNORANT FELLER
WHO TURNS OUT THE BOOTS IN THE GLOOM
NO FEARS ABOUT FAILIN'
JUST SITTIN' AND NAILIN'
THE IDEA IS TEMPTIN' BY GOOM!

THERE'S NOTHING I'D LIKE MORE TO DO
YOU ARE RIGHT! YOU'RE RIGHT! YOU'RE POSITIVELY RIGHT
VIEWING IT FROM YOUR POINT OF VIEW!!

HOBSON
(Spoken)

Well, it's high time you came to your senses ... a less
reasonable man might have taken a very different attitude ...

— 105 —

                         WILL
         (Sings)
BUT THEN! BUT THEN! REVIEWING IT AGAIN
WHICH IF YOU'LL PERMIT ME TO DO
YOUR DEAL I FEEL IS TOO GOOD TO BE REAL
BUT I'VE GOT A DEAL FOR YOU

YOUR BUSINESS IS BAD AS CAN BE, SIR
YOUR LOSSES TREMENDOUSLY LARGE
IT'S NOT NEAR A STEP-WORTH
JUST ONE MRS. HEPWORTH
WHO'LL COME BACK ONCE I'VE TAKEN CHARGE

AND MAGGIE'S NOW WORKING FOR ME, SIR
BETWEEN US WE'LL MAKE THE WHEELS SPIN
THERE'S MUCH TO MAKE OVER
AND YES I'LL TAKE OVER
FOR HALF OF WHATEVER COMES IN!!

                         HOBSON
Half ... !

                         WILL
         (Sings)
THE NAME OF THE STORE CHANGES TOO.

                         HOBSON
         (Spoken)
The name ... ?!

                         WILL
         (Sings)
YOU ARE RIGHT! YOU'RE RIGHT! YOU'RE ABSOLUTELY RIGHT
'CEPT FOR THIS I DON'T NEED YOU!!

HOBSON	WILL
Why, you impudent popinjay,	That is my final proposition
trying to steal my business!	and I will not change it.
I'd sooner walk through	Watch your language, Mr.
street stark naked ...	Hobson ... in front of my
	wife!

         (MAGGIE crosses and steps between
         them)

Piano Score No. 18A
Page 232

                         MAGGIE
Just a minute, just a minute. You'll both hold your tempers
before we continue to discuss this.
         (Sings to HOBSON)
I KNOW THE PERCENTAGE SEEMS TROUBELY
SO SILLY IT NEAR MADE YOU LAUGH
BUT FIGURE ONE QUARTER
BELONGS TO YOUR DAUGHTER
AND YOU FATHER WIND UP WITH HALF

                        — 106 —

                         HOBSON
              (Spoken, considering it)
That's three quarters ...

                         MAGGIE
              (Sings to BOTH)
AND AS FOR THE NAMES USE THEM DOUBELY
SOME PAINT FIXES THAT IN A WINK
              (To HOBSON)
WHILE WILL HAS THE BOTHER
YOUR MAIN FUNCTION FATHER
IS SIT IN MOONRAKER'S AND -- THINK!

                         HOBSON
              (Spoken)
That's not a bad idea.

                         MAGGIE
              (Sings to BOTH)
HOBSON AND MOSSOP WILL DO!

                         WILL
              (Speaks)
Hobson and Mossop?

                         MAGGIE
Aye ...

                         WILL
The name on the store will be Hobson and Mossop?

                         MAGGIE
It will ...

                         WILL
              (Sings)
IT WON'T!

                         MAGGIE
IT WON'T?

                         WILL
I WON'T HEAR ANY MORE
MOSSOP'S WHAT IT SAYS ON THIS DOOR
AND NOT FOR LESS,
WILL I LEAVE THIS ADDRESS
IT'S MOSSOP AND THEN HOBSON, OR ...

                         MAGGIE
              (Spoken)
Or, Will ... ?

                         WILL
                (Spoken)
Boots is what makes the business and I am what makes the
boots!

                         MAGGIE
                (Sings to HOBSON)
HE'S RIGHT! HE'S RIGHT!

                         WILL
YOU'RE GODDAMN RIGHT I'M RIGHT!!!

                         MAGGIE
VIEWING IT FROM HIS POINT OF VIEW

                         HOBSON
                (Speaks, crossing to door)
It's ridiculous ... out of the question ... !

                         WILL
                (Sings)
VIEWING IT FROM MY POINT OF VIEW!

                         HOBSON
Will Mossop ... you've forgotten who you are and where you
belong and a man who does that chooses the road to disgrace
and catastrophe.
                (HE goes to the door)
So, in order not to deny myself the great pleasure of
witnessing your downfall at first hand ... I agree to your
preposterous conditions!
                (HOBSON goes)

                         MAGGIE & WILL
                (Sing)
VIEWING IT FROM OUR POINT OF VIEW.

                         WILL
                (Amazed)
We won, Miss Maggie ... We won.

                         MAGGIE
Aye, that you did, Will.

                         WILL
I hope I wasn't too hard on him ...

                         MAGGIE
You spoke your mind. I'm proud of you.
                (SHE looks at him with admiration.
                HE reacts rather sheepishly. SHE
                looks significantly at the bedroom
                door)
Well ...

                        — 108 —

                    WILL
Well, I'll just clear these things away.
          (Clears things from table. Then
          returns and sits)

                    MAGGIE
Well, I'm for bed.

                    WILL
          (Warding off the inevitable)
I'll get my slate.
          (HE picks up the slate and sits)

                    MAGGIE
What ... tonight?
          (MAGGIE reacts to his reluctance,
          then goes into the bedroom. WILL
          wipes the slate and calls off)

                    WILL
You always say "Good habits are made by finding no
exceptions."
          (Calls)
What shall I write?

                    MAGGIE
          (Off)
What did you write last night?

                    WILL
"Men build houses. Love builds the home." You gave me
that.

                    MAGGIE
          (Off)   Piano Score No. 19
Tonight you think of something.   Page 239

          (WILL struggles, thinking for several
          moments. MAGGIE comes to the door
          carrying WILL's nightshirt. WILL
          turns)

                    WILL
Nought comes to me.

                    MAGGIE
It will. Give it a minute. Then come to bed. Here.
          (SHE puts nightshirt over the chair.
          Again WILL reacts reluctantly.
          MAGGIE notices and goes back into
          the bedroom)

                    WILL
          (Sings)
I DON'T THINK I'M IN LOVE ...

(MUSIC under as WILL removes his
jacket revealing a false dickie
and collar and celluloid cuffs.
Then HE takes off his trousers,
and stands there in his long underwear. Suddenly HE stops undressing,
and sings)

WILL (Continued)
FROM THE START SHE TOLD ME WHERE I WAS HEADED
TOLD ME I'D BE HERS ONCE SHE GOT ME WEDDED ... BEDDED ...
(HE hurriedly starts to dress. HE
breaks off as MAGGIE comes out of
the bedroom. SHE is wearing a hat
and carrying a valise. WILL watches
her in amazement)
Where are you going, Miss Maggie ...

MAGGIE
I'm going back to Hobson's, Will.

WILL
But we're not due there till tomorrow morning ...

MAGGIE
You don't understand, Will. I'm going back alone. You're
to stay here ... in your own shop ...

WILL
You mean, we're not ...

MAGGIE
Will, you're afraid of me ... And I can't stand having you
feel that way about me. You once said we'd have nothing
without love ... and you were right. I hoped it would
come ...

WILL
But, Miss Maggie ...

MAGGIE
We tried ... and ... at least you'll have your own shop, and
every time I come down this street and I see your name up
on that sign, I'll feel good and warm inside, knowing that
I played some part in your life ...

WILL
You're giving up, then ...

MAGGIE
I always thought marriage was just another kind of partnership. Well, it's not. It's something very different ...
something you can't just make happen ... something I just
haven't ... I just don't ...

(SHE stops. For the first time torn
by emotion so that SHE can't go on.
The lights change on her ... a rosy
glow)

WILL

I'm grateful for all you've done for me.

MAGGIE

No need for that, Willie ...

WILL

... and I admire you ...

MAGGIE

You're very kind ...

WILL

... and I've learned a lot from you ...

MAGGIE

Thank you ...

WILL

... and I don't think I can live without you.

(MAGGIE stands transfixed) Piano Score No. 19A
 Page 244

... seeing you there at the door with your hat on ... it's
like seeing a little girl walking away from a birthday party.
It's the first time I've seen you this way, Maggie. Here am
I ... standing in my underwear ... and you with your hat on.
We make an odd pair, don't we?

(MAGGIE nods) Piano Score No. 20
 Page 246

... well, odd or not ... we are a pair, Maggie. You're not
to leave me. I won't have it. It's against my wishes.
(WILL takes MAGGIE in his arms and
really kisses her. Takes the suit-
case from her and gets his nightshirt,
slings it over his shoulder and crosses
to the bedroom door. HE stops in the
doorway and turns to her.

Gruffly)
Come on, lass.
(HE goes into the bedroom. MAGGIE looks
after him in wonder. Then SHE starts to
take the hatpin out of her hat)

MAGGIE

Well, by gum ...

END

PROP LIST

I-1 MOONRAKERS

15 Steins on bar   2 Blue rosettes (Beenstock - UR)
4 Steins L winch
Table and 4 chairs L winch
1 Chair in flip
1 Chair US
2 Beenstock Boards UR
Time bell (on bar)

I-2 BOOTERY

Calling card (Mrs. Hepworth - R)
1 Pound note (Freddie - L)
Box of brass rings w/Maggie's ring (desk drawer)
Cash box (top of desk)
Ledger (on desk)
Ink well and quill pen (on desk)
Umbrella stand with 2 dust cloths (UR)
Shoes for Freddie (on counter)
Clogs (on counter)
Buckle shoes (under desk)

I-3 HOBSON'S CELLAR

2 Shoe stands (elevator)
2 Hammers (elevator)
2 Pair shoes (elevator)
2 Stools (elevator)

I-4 MOONRAKERS

4 Chairs and table (L winch)
2 Chairs (in flip)
3 Chairs (US)
2 Steins (L winch)
3 Steins (US table)
10 Steins (behind bar)
Temperance folders (Beenstock - UR)
Pipe (Lanti)

I-5 RIVER

Park bench (on elevator)

I-6 POORTOWN

Box (L)
Tub (L)
Barrel, medium tub, and small tub telescoped (UR)
Wheelbarrow with tub (UR)
Large box (DR)
Small tub (DR)
Black valise (DL)

I-7 ALLEY

Black valise (from I-6)

I-8 BOOTERY

Hobson's slippers (UR - Alice)
Marriage contract (UR - Hobson)
Dust cover (over counter)

II-1 MRS. HEPWORTH'S

Lorgnette (R - Mrs. Hepworth)
Calling card (L - Will)

II-2 CELLAR

Shop sign (R - Will)
Money bag with two pound notes (R - Will)
Shopping list (Maggie - in her Act II purse)
Window blinds tied to board (on floor)
Crate (on floor)
Sawhorse (on floor)
Bucket (on floor)
Break-away window curtain (window)
Broken chair (on floor)

II-3 FLAT IRON MARKET

Will's cart (DR)
Grandfather clock (DL)
Chair with items attached (UR - Will)
Baby carriage (DR - Wallace)
Rug cart (UR)
Pots and pans cart (UR)
Fabric cart (UL)
Rug over Bootery sign (Pre-set from UR)

II-4 CELLAR

Spool of thread with threaded needle (R end of table)
Slate, chalk and eraser (C of table)
Boot laces in box (on sink)
Penny (UL - Customer)
Monkey wrench (UL - Will)
Will's duplicate coat (R end of table)
Will's duplicate scarf (C of table)
Sewing basket (R end of table)

II-5 MOONRAKERS

3 Steins on bar
Whiskey bottle and plastic glass (L winch)
3 Whiskey bottles behind bar
2 Packs of handbills (DL - Boy)
2 Shillings (DL - Hobson)
Bar rag (on bar)
Rattle pan (Devil - elevator)
3 Trick canes (Siretta - trap, Garry - elevator, Block
                                                    - DL)
Trick banana (DL - Block)

II-6 STREET

Trick cane (hand to Hobson DL portal)
Danger sign on chain and poles (elevator)

II-7 BOOTERY

String of shoes (US shelves)
Threepence (L - Maggie)
Pad and pencil (on counter)
3 Dust covers
Sheet of leather (on wall UR)
Shoe and leather knife (in trap)
Maggie's ring (in drawer from I-2)

II-8 GRAIN ELEVATOR

Blue writ (DL - Albert)
Safety pin (DL - Freddie)
Sacks on elevator

II-9 CELLAR

On table: Wedding cake
           Cake knife
           1 Plate
           Teapot
           7 Cups and saucers
Blue writ (Hobson - from II-8)
Blue rosette (Beenstock - L)
Slate, chalk, and eraser (UR on set)
Nightshirt (L - Maggie)
Valise (L - Maggie)